TINSEL TOWN

HOLLY SCHINDLER

Welcome to Ruby's Place
Where the Christmas Spirit is Alive and Well

WE ALL HAVE ONE. Maybe it's a grandparents' house or a pond where you once skated in the winter. Maybe it's the downtown block where, on a fateful December shopping trip, you first crossed paths with your future fiancé. Or the city where you celebrated your own child's first holiday season. It's the place where Christmas comes alive, where the spirit hits you, lifts you and makes your heart believe all over again. The air isn't filled with snowflakes but flecks of magic. The impossible is possible.

That's Ruby's Place—the bar (ahem, *supper club*)—located in the tiny town of Sullivan, Missouri.

In Ruby's Place, the Christmas memories aren't just strong. They actually come to life again.

I got the idea for the series years ago, while watching the local news. What caught my attention, oddly enough, was a story on smoking ordinances in public places. Featured was a local bar owner, who insisted that prohibiting smoking throughout the city would drive her out of business. She said she was really good at doing one thing, and that was running her bar.

There was just something about the image of her face looking out of the plate glass window of her establishment. It stuck with me. Eventually, I began to wonder, *What if I wrote about a woman who was so good at running her bar, she was still there, years after her own passing?*

I published *Christmas at Ruby's* in 2017, with the idea that the short piece would stand alone.

But in 2018, I found that I wanted to go back. I wanted to spend more time with Ruby and the regulars that gathered each evening. I wanted to find out what had become of Angela, who had spent the Christmas Eves of her girlhood at Ruby's, and in *Christmas at Ruby's*, vowed to purchase the old place.

Mostly, I wanted to go back because, in a way, Ruby's had already become the place where I could tap into that Christmas spirit.

I wrote *I Remember You* in 2018, then *Sentimental Journey* in 2019. In 2020, *The Gift That Is Ruby's Place* was initially intended to close the series.

But I'd just left so much untold story on the table. Especially the backstory of Ruby herself. How *did* she decide to open that namesake supper club? Why Sullivan? What drew her back home? In 2021, I decided to answer some of those questions in *Ruby's Story*. Writing it, I also told the tale of how Roy Weber, a fellow Sullivan business owner, came to be Ruby's very first regular. And so began the *Ruby's Regulars* series spinoff. Each year, I delve into the life of one of the faces that had, during the supper club's heyday, frequented Ruby's at happy hour—and still do, each night, long after their demise.

In 2022, the regular who took center stage in *Rare Gems* was Elizabeth, Ruby's best friend. This year, in *Tinsel Town*, it's Walter, the banker who initially granted Ruby the loan she needed to open her supper club and fulfill her dream.

Next year?

All I know is that I'll be back. I cannot wait to throw open that bright green door on the front of Ruby's and reacquaint myself with the memories it still holds.

Look at that. The red neon Ruby's Place sign is glowing right now. If you stop and turn your head upward, you'll see it cutting into the darkness.

I'll meet you inside.

—*Holly Schindler*

In Memoriam

ONE BRIGHT SUNNY MORNING (or perhaps it was raining?), an obituary appeared in *The Sullivan Morning Tribune*. Which, of course, was not in itself an oddity. Even in a town as relatively small as Sullivan, Missouri, you could count on more than one appearing in each morning edition—the sad departings of kind faces never to be seen again.

What made this particular obituary stand out, one fine June morning (or maybe it was February?), was that it was not for a person. It was for a business.

Ruby's Place, the bar and eatery that had washed the sky red with its warm neon welcome since the mid-1950s, was no more. A Closed sign had been placed in the window. Its neon had been turned off for good.

Ruby Westbrook had herself been an entry in the obituary column two years prior. (Or had it been three? Four?) At any rate, by that point, the only folks left who remembered firsthand how Ruby had returned to town a retired ballerina with the somewhat unexpected (some said harebrained) plan to open a bar were grandparents. Great-grandparents, some of them. And, as everyone in this shrinking group had been commenting since her passing, her namesake establishment hadn't been the same without her. A distant family member who had swooped in to take the place over just couldn't keep it running.

But then again, some wondered, *was* it a fault of the new owner? Or was it simply that Sullivan itself had changed? Had Sullivan (as the younger residents claimed) become a more modern town, a town that did not need fussy linen tablecloths and chandeliers? A town that would rather strike out and do something new than trot out the same tired tradition yet again?

One thing had been certain: regardless of the reason, people were not coming out to Ruby's Place. Not even on Christmas Eve, which had always been Ruby's shining moment every calendar year. Once, very nearly the entire town traipsed in and out of Ruby's Place on Christmas Eve. They came to sing, to exchange gifts. They came in their absolute finest—their silk shirts and gold cuff links, their heirloom pearl necklaces and the perfume they saved for only the best occasions. They came in waves—the early revelers who arrived before the dinner hour, those who showed up after nine, and those who aimed to raise a toast on midnight so that they could wish Ruby an official Merry Christmas morning before kissing her cheek and letting her lock up for the holiday.

A constant swinging of the bright green front door had ushered the townspeople in and out. All Christmas Eve. Even the children were encouraged to come, and were served homemade marshmallows and hot cocoa, a famous specialty of Ruby's.

Come to think of it, they all admitted, rattling the

obituary page and deciding to take that second cup of coffee after all, the numbers, sadly, had been tapering off even before Ruby was gone.

After her demise? It was over. Completely. The bar… (Then again, *was* it really a bar? Didn't Ruby call it something else? What was it? Not a bar but a—*supper club!* That was it. A supper club, one to which every single resident of Sullivan was automatically a member.) Anyway, Ruby's had even closed early last Christmas Eve.

And now?

Dead, the obituary for Ruby's Place proclaimed. The heart of the old former favorite had stopped beating.

One of the strangest parts of the obituary (even stranger, some thought, than the fact that it was about a building) was that no one knew who wrote it. Betty (or was it Anna?), the *Morning Tribune* employee tasked with collecting photos and funeral details, claimed *she* would certainly never write such a preposterous thing, and had not seen the obituary before the paper had gone to print.

A small few who felt a bit guilty about letting their old gathering spot slip away gathered together on the sidewalk the night after the obituary's appearance. They cracked into a bottle of champagne and toasted Ruby's Place, now a darkened, empty building. They came, as people always came to a funeral, to say what they wished they'd said when they still had a chance: *You were so important to me.*

In the snow (or was that warm summer moonlight?) their glasses clinked—not in merriment, but in reverence.

So many details are hard to find again once time has done its work, making years gone look hazier and hazier. Decades down the road, it's hard to remember all the finer points of anything, even something as once-in-a-lifetime as an obituary for a business. Imagine—not being able to remember the exact year it had appeared (was it '93? Or '95?), or the season, or who, exactly, had made that trek to the street outside to raise that final glass.

Part of the town's forgetting stemmed from the fact that it did not seem, right then, after dark, as glasses were being raised, that something had been lost. It did not seem, at that moment, that something would always be missing. It did not seem that a hole had formed. It only seemed that a chapter had come to a close.

Slowly, as the people of Sullivan began the work of moving on, it wasn't just the obituary that grew hazy in their minds. Their memories of Ruby's Place lost their detail, too. They turned gauzy and gray and indistinct. Had Ruby's opened in the '50s or '60s? What *was* the name of that old friend of hers, the one who showed up every night for happy hour? Could anyone remember the songs sung before closing time?

No. They couldn't. Ruby's Place had turned into a smear in their minds. Decades later, in the midst of the holiday bustle, shoppers might occasionally pause in front of the long-empty, derelict building. As snow gathered on their shoulders and their noses turned ever pinker, they'd look right into the old place, and they'd have to ask themselves:

How old was I when I first went to Ruby's? Eight? Ten?

What was the color of that beautiful velvet dress I talked Mom into buying for one big night out?

What was the name of my date, the one who took me there one Christmas Eve?

Ruby let me take home the mistletoe I was standing under for my very first kiss. I pressed it in a book…but what happened to it?

They'd forgotten. All of them.

Well. They'd forgotten all but one thing. One small, singular detail rang out clearly in every single memory of every single person who had ever spent a Christmas Eve in Ruby's:

They remembered Ruby's homemade marshmallows and cocoa.

Because, as everyone knows, you never do forget something sweet.

1.

DECEMBER 24, 2018

IN THE DARKNESS OF THE CLOSED BANK, with snow falling on the other side of his office window and the holiday beckoning him, Scott Drummond scowled like a regular Scrooge. The same Scott Drummond who in previous years had been known to all in his hometown of Sullivan, Missouri as the merriest of them all. Tonight, Scott scowled at the date on his desk calendar. He scowled at the sound of the decorative silver bells that jingled in the wind all down the street outside. And he scowled at the tiny fake tree nestled between his old-school inbox and his phone. That poor tree was, in fact, the primary recipient of Scott's scowl. The miniature tinsel draped haphazardly across the horrendously artificial branches was looking awfully garish and out-of-date to Scott. Tarnished, even.

Not to mention used-up and trampled on.

But this was not a feeling that had only found him at that moment—after nightfall on Christmas Eve. Scott had been hunted by this gloomy, wholly uncheerful sensation all through the lead-up to the holidays. In fact, he had first felt it about his own Drummond household tinsel. The silver stuff Scott and his wife had painstakingly removed from every tree they'd ever had, all the way back to that first year after they'd exchanged their wedding vows. Each January, they'd engage in the same ritual: They'd laugh in sync while they wrapped the silver ropes around one of those hardware store plastic cord organizers. They'd pat the sparkly strands as they tucked them away—which was really a way of patting themselves on the back for another successful holiday—and call out something like, "See you next year, friend," as they pushed the cardboard storage box up into the attic.

The next November, they would race each other to the attic to officially begin the decorating season.

This year, though, on Thanksgiving weekend—always the official tree-trimming weekend for the Drummonds— Scott had, on his own, lugged the limp cardboard box down from the space between the pink stripes of attic insulation. His wife, meanwhile, engaged in some sort of wrestling match with their turkey while a mismatched assortment of in-laws blathered on in the living room, arguing about football stats.

That afternoon, Scott had tugged open the cardboard flaps only to find the metallic strands of tinsel looking pawed and crumpled, heat damaged and worn.

As the days had marched closer to Christmas, Scott had begun to realize it wasn't just his own tinsel, it was *all* tinsel. All through the town of Sullivan. It was the tinsel strung across the lobby of the bank where he served as the head of business loans. It was the tinsel strung across the shelves of The Page Turner bookstore—Scott's favorite downtown business, the one he browsed every day on his lunch hour. It was the tinsel draped in scallops on the elementary school entrance. And it was even—Scott hated himself for feeling this way— but it was the tinsel his daughter had bought with her own allowance to wrap about the antenna on his car radio. (This was a sweet gesture on Alessandra's part, a *thank you* she'd wanted to extend to her dad for taping her latest spelling test to the glove compartment in his car, where he could see it every day. Alessandra was a horrendous speller, almost comical, and that A was as good as an Oscar.)

His sourness had continued to bleed outward, extending to the aluminum snowflakes that city council had been pinning to the streetlights all throughout the downtown area for decades—since the '50s, some of the old-timers swore, pointing to the sharp creases and asking, *Doesn't that just remind you of the fins on the back of an old Belair?* Why, Scott was even put off by the twinkle lights on front yard trees.

Really—*twinkle lights!*

He didn't like feeling this way. It was entirely out of character for him—for Scott Drummond, of all people, who had always before, every December, shouted greetings of "H*aaaaa*ppy holidays!" to every familiar face he bumped into on his way from his reserved parking space to the front door of the bank. Scott Drummond, who had taken up his father's habit of keeping small wrapped candy canes in his pockets for every child who skipped across his path. Scott Drummond, whose trunk was perpetually brimming with boxes wrapped in shiny paper.

And yet, in the last few days, frowns had even been jumping onto Scott's face during weekday commutes should a carol have the audacity to come on the radio yet *again*.

It was beyond his control, he tried to assure himself. It was something that age brought, right on time, along with bifocals and creaky knees. The gaudy, fake side of Christmas appealed to children. But after a good four decades of the on-slaught, it began to smack you, and you flinched before you could stop yourself. It was the swing of the knee after being whacked with a reflex hammer. It just *happened.*

This line of reasoning was sound in the abstract, but it made him squirm all the same. Because it didn't explain why all this *bah-humbug*-ness on his part also seemed to apply to egg nog (his favorite holiday treat) and cozy evenings at home. Why he had actually grimaced at the black and white screen during their annual viewing of *It's a Wonderful Life.* Christmas, this year—yes, the actual holiday itself—seemed wrung-out and stained and muddied. Like the wet, wrecked jackets his boys threw on the front hall floor every time they came home from sledding.

Scott ached to confess these feelings. But to whom? His wife, Jennifer, would have taken Scott's feelings person-ally, seen it as a sign of boredom creeping into the space be-tween them. And anyone else would have surely just brushed it off, or said something generic and unhelpful—maybe sighed wistfully and claimed melancholy was a funny thing; it infected you inexplicably and seemed nearly impossible to treat.

And anyway, Scott didn't need an answer. Scott already knew the answer. Scott Drummond was a practical man, a man of numbers and logic who could easily recognize right answers. Since the earliest days of his childhood, Scott had always been able to add long streams of numbers in his head. And this stream of—well, not exactly numbers, but repeating patterns of disappointment—all added up to the same thing:

He was missing his father. Walter. The same Walter in the picture on the corner of Scott's desk. The same Walter whose portrait still hung near the ancient vault that no one could remember how to open, because he had once been the VP of the Bank of Sullivan. The very same bank where Scott now worked. Every single workday, Scott would pass by that old portrait of his dad and he would find himself wishing, with everything he had, for one more Christmas Eve with him. One more of their special nights at Ruby's Place, just the two of them.

The desire had only grown stronger as time had inched closer to Christmas.

How—odd, really. To be missing his father. After all this time. Nearly thirty years after his death. The ache had crashed against his chest as he'd carved Jennifer's Thanksgiving turkey. Attacked him with such force that he felt caught up in some angry creature's jaws. And it had not let up since.

"You still here?" a voice called out from Scott's open office door.

Scott jumped, glancing up to find out who had interrupted his somber Christmas Eve.

2.

BRIAN YOUNG SHOULD HAVE DRIVEN out of Sullivan an hour ago. Right after shaking Scott Drummond's hand at the bank, wishing him a happy holiday, and thanking him for that one last meeting before his Christmas Eve kicked into gear. But here Brian was, still circling through the streets of town, over and over again.

"Not *one*," he muttered with disgust. "Not a single one."

The *one* to which he referred was a hotel. Or a motel. Or a bed and breakfast. Or—

He found himself letting out a short, breathy sigh that could double for a chuckle of utter disbelief. "On Christmas," he said. "No room at the inn."

It was ironic, he caught himself thinking. But also not exactly accurate. There was no room at the inn because there *were no inns*. Not one. Not inside the town limits, anyway. He'd thought surely he'd be able to find a place with no problem. A single man, on his own, no family to speak of. He only needed one bed. Why, a cot or a couch would do. He had looked forward to it, actually. A quiet holiday in a quaint small town.

Yes, a small-town Christmas. Like something out of a Hallmark card. He would wake on Christmas morning, and it wouldn't matter that he was alone, because he would be greeted by smiling faces in the lobby of wherever it was he had decided to stay, and he would be offered complimentary coffee with hazelnut flavoring, and *Please, Mr. Young, don't spend the morning cooped up in your room. Why, I've got chocolate pecan sticky buns from scratch in the oven. I always make them for our guests on Christmas morning, and we gather here and talk and pass the paper around like we're old friends. Later, we'll go sledding with the rest of the kids and for dinner, we'll head to the First Baptist, where there's a special feast planned for those who don't cook. The tables stretch all the way across the room; it feels like having half the town over for supper!*

Or something to that effect.

Brian was not from Sullivan originally, but his father and grandfather had grown up in tiny Midwest towns. His grandfather had told him the long and winding tale of being forced, as a young boy, to visit his cousins up in St. Louis, and being utterly dismayed that Saturday nights were not the grand events they'd been at the square back home, where literally *everyone* came out and milled about, chatting and having treats and watching movies and eating ice cream and "just generally horsing around," as his granddad had put it. He could not believe that in the city, folks kept to themselves. "What do you even *do* in the city?" he'd wound up asking his cousin, his voice tinged with such exasperation that the tale had instantly become family lore. You could bet that *somebody* at the family reunion was going to reenact the scene, going over-the-top enough to clutch their hair in a fist.

The rest of the family had laughed, but Brian had always marveled at his grandfather's small-town Saturdays. To think of a square so full of—well—everyone—that you never once felt lonely. Even in a town of a hundred people total.

It sounded like heaven.

He had hoped Sullivan would be such a place. It would not seem, then, a horrible thing at all to have to be working on Christmas, hammering out the details of the Bank of Sullivan's demolition and rebuild.

Early last fall, he had been called (as an employee for one of the biggest developers in Missouri) by one of the members of the Sullivan City Council, and warned, "There'll be blowback." No one in Sullivan would cotton to the idea of knocking down something so old, something that had been part of their lives for so long.

That's what the councilman had said, anyway. Brian had taken him at his word, spending the better part of two months on a proposal that could please even the most reluctant of Sullivanites.

In the end, though? Nothing. Not one gripe or complaint. The only people who'd come to the public meeting were a somewhat nosy elderly couple and a few owners of already-existing downtown businesses (Rob from The Page Turner bookstore, Tina from the It Ain't Over Yet flea market) who had liked the idea of renovating a building so close to their own shops. The beginning of bringing traffic downtown, or so they'd thought.

It had disappointed Brian. Not because he'd been geared up for a fight, but because he had grown so tired of just knocking things down. He hadn't realized how much he'd wanted someone to refuse until the refusal hadn't come. Besides, there was a vault deep in the center of the bank—an ancient one, unused these days, with one of those giant spinning combinations and a heavy door. Frozen completely shut. Logic said it was empty, sure, but wasn't anyone the least bit curious? Didn't they have a sense of imagination about it? Didn't they want to crack into it before committing to demolition?

Twenty-five years into his career, Brian felt a little like a destructive jerk—the annoying little brother careening into the tower of blocks his sister had labored over for an entire afternoon.

Oh, he knew that the bricks and the mortar were just the outer shell. It was the inside of a building that was important.

Only, where did *that* go, once it didn't have any bricks to keep it contained anymore? Was there some ascension for a building's soul, the same as there was for a human's?

Brian's headlights fell on the front of an old Victorian house. Not in good shape—not at all. In fact, he could imagine ghost hunters hauling their gadgets up the front steps to film one of their cell-phone documentaries about the place, making up wild tales about the creaking stairs and the groaning floorboards.

Brian didn't see horror stories, though. He saw potential. This was exactly the kind of place that should be saved before it fell in.

He unlatched his seat belt and trudged up the crumbling front walk. Behind him, his car idled and his headlights continued to illuminate the front door.

His heart actually ached for the place. Which was odd. Some old house he'd never seen before in his life. And he was having the same feeling about the place that someone might have seeing their own childhood home designated condemned and scheduled for demolition.

Don't worry. I'll save you.

Brian reached his hand out to touch the porch railing.

"You!" came a shout. "What're you doing here?"

Brian flinched as a floodlight attacked him.

3.

WHEN THE UNMISTAKABLE RATTLE and roar announced the city snowplow had returned for a second round, clearing the street outside her door mere minutes from her official opening time, Angela grabbed her lucky hat and lunged for the door.

"Thank you!" she shouted from the entrance, extending her arm and waving her hand back and forth, sweeping widely over her head. "Thank you for coming back! On the house—a free—"

But the driver of the snowplow didn't hear her. Or, maybe, had no use for a hot toddy on Christmas Eve. Maybe all he wanted to do was hurry up and get this drive over with so he could go home.

Angela hugged herself, the scratchy wool of the ugliest mud-brown knit hat on the planet making her forehead itch.

The snowplow disappeared around the corner, leaving Angela alone on the snowy sidewalk.

She turned, reaching for the door that had fallen shut behind her, the one she had freshly painted with the same bright green she remembered from her childhood. The shade

Ruby herself had always used.

But before she could slip inside, she caught sight of her reflection in the plate glass window. There she was, the same old Angela. Grayer and heavier and ten years older than she wished she was, worry engulfing her face.

As she stared, the details of the past year danced about her, like flakes of falling snow.

It had been one year ago to the day when a lonely Angela had returned to Sullivan. As she'd walked the downtown streets, a cardinal had clipped her head, knocking that lucky hat of hers to the sidewalk. After retrieving it and shaking it free of a few wet clumps of snow, Angela had found herself right there, in that very spot, right outside of Ruby's old entrance.

A year ago, she'd stared through the grimy front window of the long-gone Ruby's Place, thinking for the first time in ages of her Aunt Elizabeth, that movie star of a woman with her blond updo and red nails, who had brought a young Angela to Ruby's Place every Christmas Eve. Angela had looked forward to their nights together, which were always proceeded by the arrival of a white garment box from Elizabeth's dress store. Angela would peel the paper back to find that Aunt Elizabeth had supplied her with pretty party dresses and sparkly rhinestone jewelry, designer coats, and even her first pair of heels (long before her mother wanted her to have them).

But the memories didn't stop there. Standing in front of Ruby's, the entirety of those long-gone Christmas Eves had come back to life for her—the crowds with their arms draped around each other's necks, voices soaring as they belted Christmas carols loud enough to drown out the sounds of the piano. She remembered the merry holiday hellos, and how the words themselves had felt like a hug. The way her aunt had treated her as a grown up (the first time anyone in her life had). She'd recalled the enormous crystal chandelier and the silver dotting the tables, the candlelight that had flickered, leaving freckles of light to dance across happy faces.

She'd remembered Ruby's homemade marshmallows, too. Angela had been able to taste them just by looking inside.

She'd ached to get it back—all of it. The sense of togetherness and the taste of the marshmallows and the feeling of promise and possibility that had seemed to infiltrate everything on those Ruby's Place Christmas Eves. So much so, she'd soon found herself on the other side of Scott Drummond's desk at the Bank of Sullivan, presenting him with her idea to renovate Ruby's Place. Bring it back to its old glory.

She had never been a fidgeter, but that day, she hadn't been able to quit squirming in the chair across from Scott. She'd wondered how a childhood friend could have made her so nervous. Then again, she'd thought, maybe it was the suit she wore that she only sort of liked. Still an out-of-town visitor, Angela'd had to scour the racks for something professional to wear, cursing Sullivan's only clothing store for not being her Aunt Elizabeth's shop. The hangers had screeched as she'd shopped, angry to be pushed aside. She'd finally found something that worked—not something she loved, though, which she tried to tell herself contributed to her discomfort during her meeting with Scott. There she sat, sweating through her jacket, her lucky hat wadded up and shoved into her purse.

Scott had stared at her for the longest time, eyes wide and unblinking. Later, he would tell her that the stare was only because her proposal had seemed too good to be true. So too-good, he'd worried that if he did blink, the vision of her there would disappear, show itself to be the mirage it really was.

Angela, though, hadn't seen excitement during their meeting. He'd seemed distant. Almost detached from the idea. So when his answer finally came, she'd wondered if she'd heard him right.

"Yes," he'd said.

"Yes—what?"

"Yes to all of it."

But the *all of it* was really only the sketchiest of propositions. Reopen the old Ruby's Place. Bring it back, renovate it to make it look like it always had. "Do I—" Angela had tried to swallow, but her mouth was too dry. "Do I—need a—business plan or something?"

"No, this is fine," Scott had said, his fingers already hammering about on his keyboard. "All the plan you need."

It can't be that easy—can it? Angela had wondered. "It must—it must cost more for what I have in mind. More to renovate than simply knock it down," she'd said.

"Probably," he'd agreed.

That was not the Scott Drummond Angela had always known. Scott was not exactly a cold fish; when they had greeted each other in his office, he had shown her pictures of his family in such a way that she imagined he kissed those kids of his at every opportunity. In the course of their *nice to see you again* conversation, he had referred to his wife as his "sweetheart" twice. But Angela had never known him to make a decision solely on sentimentality. Not once. Scott Drummond had always been practical. Even in the first grade.

She'd wondered: Was she taking advantage of an old friend?

But as he'd begun to tell her about some of the problems the old building had had—about the mold and the rot and the infestations that had discouraged everyone else—she had wondered if he was taking advantage of her.

"Maybe—I'm not—I'm no expert. Or—I've never even renovated so much as a bathroom!" Angela had exclaimed, leaning forward to gather her purse.

She had started to back out, thanking him for his time. But Scott had reached across his desk to keep her from getting up and leaving. "Nobody's been able to make it work because nobody loves it like you," he'd told her.

"Why, Scott Drummond," she'd said, "you're turning into a maudlin old sap."

And they had dissolved into laughter.

The laughter had followed the two of them for a year, as renovations had taken place. Scott had refused to come inside anytime she'd invited him, telling her he didn't want to see it before the grand unveiling. But it had been a shared, unspoken excitement when they'd encountered each other in the market or on the street outside of the bank.

Now, a full year and many tens of thousands of dollars into a renovation, on this, her opening night, Angela glanced up and down the street.

Sullivan's downtown remained painfully empty. It had cleared out with the closing of the last shop, and the quiet in the air—Angela could detect not a single voice or car engine—indicated no one was planning on coming back.

Not yet, anyway, Angela tried to tell herself.

Maybe not ever, she added.

Angela wondered if she'd gotten everything all mixed up. Maybe those warm, lovely feelings she'd associated with Ruby's Place hadn't really been about the old supper club at all. Maybe they had simply been the most common feelings of youth, that time before a person had ever had a chance to fail.

At her feet, a cardinal hopped forward a few steps. He cocked his head as he stared up at her. He had a kind of knowing way about him—almost human. She half-expected him to break into a round of "White Christmas."

"Did we meet here last year?" she grumbled. "Cardinals appear when angels are near, right? Isn't that the old saying?"

She shook her head, pointing at the quiet street. "Where are my guardian angels now, huh?"

What had she done? How could she be so certain this town would want to revisit the past?

How could Scott Drummond have granted her such an enormous loan? How could he have been so blind to the ludicrousness of her idea? Resurrect Ruby's Place from the dead. *Really.* Nothing ever came back from the dead. Once it was gone, it was gone.

And Ruby's Place, she recalled, had already been put to bed in *The Sullivan Morning Tribune*'s obituary column.

Her forehead itched. *Some lucky hat,* she grumbled to herself.

"I think I've made the biggest mistake of my life," Angela confessed to the bird.

Not exactly the kind of epiphany one hoped to have on Christmas Eve.

4.

BACK AT THE BANK, Scott was still trying to get his head together enough to find an answer to the question that had been lobbed at him from his open office doorway.

Before he could, though, Gregory repeated, "What are you doing still here?"

Scott wondered how he could have been so surprised by Gregory's appearance. He knew Gregory was in the bank somewhere, doing his after-hours cleaning. The cart carrying his supplies should have warned Scott he was getting closer. Gregory did have the squeakiest janitor's supply cart in existence.

Oh, come on, Scott chastised himself. *You know exactly how Gregory could have sneaked up on you.* It was because he had been lost deep in thought, his conscience zeroed in on only the sound of the clock on his office wall. That second hand had been *tsk-tsk*ing him for the last hour, echoing through the stillness of the bank. In fact, Scott had just been thinking with annoyance that the second hand was getting increasingly louder, almost like an old radio that increased in volume the longer it had a chance to warm up.

Gregory frowned at him, echoing everything the clock had been chastising him for when he remarked, "Dragging your feet about leaving, hours after closing? And here it is Christmas Eve?"

It was quite the formal name, Scott caught himself thinking, as he had dozens of times. *Especially for a janitor,* his brain added, even though he knew better. What did that even mean, anyway? A formal name wasn't appropriate for a man whose job didn't require a tie?

From day one, Gregory had assumed the role of the bank's in-house philosopher. At first, Scott had quietly chuckled to himself anytime Gregory tossed out words like *quandary* or *ethos* or told Scott that they got along so well because Gregory, too, was quite the pragmatist. But when Gregory'd managed to work Jean-Paul Sartre into a regular Wednesday morning conversation, Scott had asked him flat-out what the big idea was. And Gregory had said, with not so much as a shrug, that he did, in fact, have a PhD in philosophy.

He had smiled at Scott, offering a wink that said his choices were his own, and it was none of Scott's business why he was in this line of work.

That night—after sunset on Christmas Eve, in the otherwise empty Bank of Sullivan—Scott stared back at Gregory, trying to remind him that he, too, was deserving of some of his own privacy. Especially on a night that should have glittered but didn't.

"Whatever you've got on your desk can't be as important as the family," Gregory persisted, ignoring Scott's expression. He squinted, trying to make out what Scott had been looking at—all those papers spread out across the top of his desk.

"What is that?" Gregory asked. "Plans for the bank

demolition? I know Mr. Young was here earlier. Burning the Christmas Eve oil, you two. I couldn't help but overhear your discussion. Is there really an old vault in this place that hasn't been opened in ages?"

"There is. No one remembers how to open it, and the combination's been lost—" Scott started. His voice trailed when he found himself unsure of how to finish the sentence. He already had strange pangs of loss associated with the old bank, and they hadn't even demolished it yet. He had this nagging suspicion that maybe they shouldn't tear it down, but clearly, he reminded himself anytime he'd considered bringing up the subject, he was the only one who felt that way.

Gregory craned his neck. "Hey," he said, surprise lacing his tone as he stared at some of the architect's renderings. "That's not the bank. That's Ruby's Place."

Scott cleared his throat and started the awkward business of hurriedly putting everything away, pretending he hadn't *really* been staring at the plans, even though the evidence was still there in plain view.

"I heard Angela was putting it all back the way it was," Gregory said.

"Y—yes. Same everything. Including the name," Scott said, his face growing ever hotter.

"Yeah, I saw the sign go up," Gregory said. "It really was an extraordinary place. Not a *bar*, exactly, but…" He tilted his head, searching for the right word.

"Supper club," Scott murmured. "Ruby always called it a supper club. Modeled after the places she'd seen during her life as a ballerina in New York."

"She owned that place forever. Mixed drinks up until her last breath, that one. And she must've been there since—"

"She opened in 1955," Scott said.

"I could believe that," Gregory said. "The place definitely had that mid-century feel to it."

"No, I know for certain—my dad—he worked here at the bank, too."

"Right. The portrait by the old vault."

"Anyway," Scott said, "he granted Ruby the loan to begin with. Talked about it a lot. 1955. It's drilled into my brain."

"A loan? To a woman? Back then? That was pretty unheard of."

"There was a community fund. Here at the bank," Scott said. "Actually, there still *is* a community fund. I used most of it to fund Angela's renovations."

"Taking up where your dad left off."

"I hadn't used that community fund since he died, believe it or not," Scott admitted. "Nothing ever felt like it fit. Dad had always been in charge of the fund, and he left instructions that it was meant to be used for special circumstances. For—oh, not exactly long shots, but for the people who were less likely to qualify. Nothing had ever seemed special enough."

"Until Angela, that is," Gregory said.

"When Angela came, I remember, I got goosebumps. Because for the first time, I thought, *If this isn't special, what is?*"

"Where'd it come from, anyway?" Gregory asked.

"The community fund? Dad said a woman in town willed all the money from her estate to form it. Dad was a boy when she died, but he remembered her somehow. I don't have any idea who managed the fund until he started working here. The details are all so fuzzy to me now. So many things you don't really listen to when you're young. But the woman's name—what was it?" Scott gnawed at his lip. "Bonwit! That's it."

Gregory frowned. "Not Hetty Bonwit."

"Yes! Hetty." Now it was Scott's turn to frown. "How did you know—"

"Hetty had no money to speak of. It couldn't have been her."

"How would you—"

"A distant relative."

"Of yours?"

Gregory nodded. "I get lost in the genealogy. It's not a straight line. She wasn't a grandmother. Maybe a three-times-great aunt? A third cousin twice removed from the uncle's father's sister's dog? Who knows. Anyway, the story's one that got passed down, one generation to another. Had a tinge of scandal, you know, which makes it the kind of thing people always want to talk about. Even when it's your own family."

Gregory grinned, letting the word—*scandal*—soak in a bit. "Her husband committed suicide right at the start of the Depression. Lost everything, you know. And Hetty—she locked herself in her house. A big old Victorian thing. Out there off Belmont."

"Oh, yeah," Scott said. "On the register of historic places. I know the place. You can't be a lifelong resident of Sullivan and not know it. Rotting on fast-forward these days, but still on its feet."

"Hetty wouldn't have anything to do with the rest of the family after her husband died," Gregory continued. "It was a mystery why. I know my grandparents were a little sad about it, like they'd always wished there was some way they could have reached her or done more. She died alone. No one had seen her for years when she went. Nobody showed for the funeral."

"Huh," Scott said. "Dad never told me any of that. Just that Hetty had left money to start the fund." He flopped back into his chair, thinking. "So weird…"

"Well," Gregory said, "some nice woman started a community fund to help the people of Sullivan, anyway. Whoever she was."

"No," Scott insisted. "I'm sure Dad said Bonwit."

"At any rate, your dad approved the loan," Gregory went on, ignoring Scott's protests. "And I bet the two of you went to Ruby's Place all the time."

"Every year on Christmas Eve," Scott said.

"Walter had a hand in it. In creating that charming little place where the entirety of Sullivan came together, everyone decked out in their absolute finest. Ruby's was always lovely, all year long—but there was something about Ruby's on Christmas, wasn't there? Almost…look, I'm usually a total cynic, but the only word that comes to mind—and I'm using it completely unsarcastically here—is magical."

Scott inhaled, like he would have against any sharp pain. In addition to the gaudy tinsel, the bank had been decked out in pine boughs, which gave his office the odd smell of a candle that had already been burned.

"My wife made Christmas reservations at a Colorado ski resort," Scott said. "Months ahead of time. I talked her out of it. I wanted to be here. I wanted—"

"—that chance to feel close to your dad again," Gregory finished. "Be close to what he helped create."

"This entire holiday, all I've thought of is him," Scott confessed.

"So you're sitting here, on Christmas Eve, afraid of not doing right by your dad," Gregory surmised. "Any business can fail. Even Ruby's Place did once. What if you invested wrong? Wasted his money? You and Angela remember it fondly—but what if nobody else does? What if nobody shows? I mean, the rumor mill *has* been swirling about the place, and usually, curiosity is enough to draw a crowd…"

"But," Scott said, encouraging Gregory to go on.

"But," Gregory said, "it *has* been snowing most of the day." He raised his chin as though it might help him get a better look out the window behind Scott's shoulder. "Might keep some from coming out to the reopening."

Scott swiveled to look out his window, too. The street was empty, no sign that anyone at all was downtown on Christmas Eve. It rattled him to realize the possibility of Angela opening Ruby's for no one. Especially if he dragged his feet enough that even his own family missed opening night.

"The thing is," Scott admitted, his face still turned toward the window, "as much as I *don't* want to go—and see, as you say, a business doomed to fail—I also want to go more than anything."

"Because?"

"I'm just so hungry for one more—anything," Scott said. Somehow, it was easier to make these confessions to the falling snow rather than Gregory's face. "One more time sledding down the biggest hill in town with him. One more of his *Don't tell your mother about this* adventures. One more—"

"—Christmas at Ruby's?"

Scott swiveled his chair to face forward again. He reached across his desk to pinch one of the branches on his small artificial tree. "It's really foolish."

"No, it's human."

"What am I supposed to do now, though? Pick up the family, go to Ruby's Place, and see that my dad's nowhere inside? Have to face the fact that I'll never feel close to him again, not even in a familiar setting? I think I'm going to step in there and miss him more than ever." Scott's eyes landed yet again on the picture at the corner of his desk.

"You might," Gregory said. When Scott turned a *thanks a lot* look his way, Gregory shrugged. "I just get it. That's all. Why you're dragging your feet, I mean. Why you're still here, going over plans and paperwork on Christmas Eve. It probably won't be easy being inside. But then again, you'll never make another memory of Ruby's unless you go. The only thing you'll feel, when you think of Ruby's, is the hole where your dad used to be. If you go tonight, regardless of what else happens, you'll have memories of your wife—how wonderful she'll look, all dolled up and smelling sweet—and your children. Years from now, when you look back on tonight, there they'll be, frozen in your mind at the sweet little maddening ages they are right now. They won't be young forever."

Scott nodded. Gregory was right, of course.

But when Scott didn't reach for his coat, Gregory asked, "There's something else, isn't there?"

The second hand continued to tick.

"The *real* fear," Gregory guessed, "is that your father will fade completely if you walk in there and make new memories without him. And the last thing you want is for that to happen."

Scott tensed as Gregory added, "Down the street, the place that holds some of your fondest memories will swing its door open and let you return. But is it ever possible to bring the past back? Or does a revisit inevitably feel like a hollow imitation?"

Scott rubbed his face, chuckling as he shook his head.

"Uncanny," he muttered.

"What, my admirable grasp of human nature?" Gregory asked, an amused smirk on his face.

"Why don't you get a little less good at sizing people up?" Scott asked.

Gregory grabbed the supply cart. "Wouldn't be my style," he said.

The cart had only barely moved forward half a squeaky inch when Gregory stopped. "Hetty Bonwit?"

"I swear that's what he said."

"I wonder why. It *couldn't* have been her." He shook his head. "At any rate, if you don't mind, I want to get your office done as quickly as I can. That way I can change and head to Ruby's myself."

5.

INSIDE RUBY'S PLACE, as Angela fretted in the kitchen, Ruby stepped up to the bar. The same bold ballerina who had opened the supper club in 1955 and run it until her death in the nineties. Here she was, her chestnut hair twisted into the bun she'd worn as a dancer, a large red glass brooch pinned just beneath the collar of her white silk blouse. She poured a scotch neat, the favorite drink of one of her favorite regulars.

As if summoned by the mere pouring of the drink, Walter Drummond appeared dressed as he always had during his favorite time of life—in a suit with wide lapels, somewhat oversized sideburns, and slight gray creeping into his otherwise dark hair. He smiled as he launched into his familiar toast.

"To the ghosts of Christmases past!" he shouted, raising his glass.

Ruby crossed her arms over her chest and glared, in no mood to tolerate Walter's legendary love of puns. "I thought you said this would be a no-brainer," she grumbled.

"Oh, Rubes, come on, now," Walter said, sliding onto a stool and picking up his drink. "What were all us regulars going to do, scare investors away forever?" He shifted on the stool, remembering the shenanigans of the regulars—those who had frequented Ruby's Place during their lifetimes and still gathered at happy hour behind the Closed sign. How they had messed with the minds of anyone a realtor happened to bring by. "Some of the things we cooked up," Walter said with a roll of his eyes. "Bees in the walls, beating the pipes—wetting the walls and the floor to make it appear as though there were leaks and mold! We were getting to be such a cliched bunch of haunts!"

Ruby clenched her jaw in annoyance.

"What?" he asked.

"I don't like that word. *Haunt.* You know that."

"Yeah, well, you and I both know this place was starting to fall into disarray all around us," Walter said. "It was getting to the point that we didn't have to pretend there were leaks or mold—there really was. We had to have someone step in to rescue the building. If it had caved in—"

"—there's no telling what would have happened to us," Ruby finished.

The "us," to which they both referred was far bigger than just the two of them, of course. Walter and Ruby were both aware that the restored supper club was brimming with those who had ever claimed the title of Ruby's regulars. They could all be heard shuffling about, anxiously awaiting the arrival of the town of Sullivan. Which was to say they anxiously awaited the arrival of their loved ones, those they had been separated from for years, the same way that Walter had been separated from his son Scott.

They paced there in the shadows, afraid that their anticipated reunions would never come to be.

Ruby's eyes glittered as she turned her face away from

the shadows and toward a large plate glass window. Snow continued to fall on the empty street. Already, it seemed as though the snowplow had never been by. "What if this was a bad idea? What if we sink Angela financially?"

"Ruby, I want you to listen to me," Walter said. "There is absolutely no chance of Angela suffering any financial hardship."

"You don't think bankruptcy would be a financial hardship?"

"Oh, Rubes, now, do you really think I'd set Angela up to fail? Not in a million years. I have this covered. Trust me."

Ruby relaxed a bit—but only a bit. "They should be here by now," she whispered, nodding once toward the street.

"They will be," Walter promised.

"How can you say that?" Ruby asked.

"I can say anything I like," Walter responded.

"Fine. How can you *assume* that," Ruby corrected herself.

"Because, I'm not done yet, Rubes," Walter told her.

"Something's happened," Ruby guessed. "I can see it in your face."

"I might have heard a fairly nasty rumor."

"You don't run on rumors," Ruby said. "If gossip found its way to you, you would find out for sure if it was true."

Walter placed his drink on the bar. He could hear the regulars shuffle nervously behind him. "They want to tear down the bank."

"Tear it down?"

"And the old vault, too."

"You told me the vault was the safest place in this town," Ruby said, looking horrified.

Vaults and banks were for special things. Valuable

things. And while every single one of the regulars had learned that, for the most part, it really was true—you couldn't take it with you—they had also learned that most of the "it" didn't matter. The only part that did—the only truly valuable item in all their lifetimes of accumulated stuff—was their memory.

It was the only important thing to leave behind—the memory of who you were.

And they had given the memories of Ruby's Place to Walter for safekeeping in his precious vault.

"I got this out of the vault before the night got under-way," Walter said, placing a small wooden box on the bar and patting it lightly.

"There's nothing worse than to be forgotten," Ruby reminded him. "Especially on Christmas."

Walter nodded, in complete agreement. "I've got what I like to call an ace in the hole," he told Ruby. "And he's on his way now."

6.

SCOTT'S SHOULDERS COLLAPSED and a disappointed grunt escaped his lips as he found his entire front door covered in row after row of tinsel. All of it secured with clumsy strips of tape. A "Merry Christmas, Daddy!" construction paper sign had been stuck in the middle of the tortured clump of silver swirls. This was exactly the kind of thing Alessandra would do to welcome him home.

It was sweet. It warmed his heart. And it made him dread the rest of the evening even more.

When he finally stepped into the living room, Jennifer flinched, tucking her phone away, pretending she hadn't been trying to call to find out why he was so late getting home. Scott was notoriously bad with his cell phone—or phones, really. A string of the cheap prepaid variety, all of them going lost or getting broken or, once, melting in the July heat in his glove compartment. He hated the intrusiveness, or so he'd always proclaimed. Which made Jennifer feel, each time she tried to get him on the phone, like she was walking in on him in the bathroom.

Scott attempted to smile an apology. "Where is everybody?" he asked, his voice too high and too loud for him to truly be happy.

The kids had been waiting far too long. They were hungry and their dress-up clothes included itchy, hot woolen Christmas sweaters, and they were starting to relieve their discomfort by punching each other.

"Come on," Scott said, using his best cheerleader voice, the one that encouraged the kids to not be afraid of the dentist or get in the pool or try the broccoli or take the cough syrup or go to the first day of school. "Let's get out of here."

And so they headed out, Jennifer and Scott herding the children into the car that hadn't even had a chance to get cold yet. Snow was continuing to fall fast enough that Scott's recent tire tracks weren't visible in his headlights. He made his way cautiously toward the downtown area, tires crunching through the inches of frozen white clumps.

Jennifer reached over from the passenger seat, laying her hand on Scott's as he gripped the gear shift. "This will be so wonderful for Angela," she said.

And right then—with glad tidings in her voice, and wearing the pearl earrings he'd bought for her on their first anniversary, with the starlight falling through the windshield to scatter like little freckles across her cheeks, with her eyes all misty—Scott almost felt it. The Christmas spirit.

Almost.

But then his seat lurched forward as the twins' wrestling match tumbled against his back.

"*Boys*," Jennifer scolded, in that mother's voice of hers. That tone all children roll their eyes against.

Alessandra sighed in her *I'm above all their shenanigans* way, which maybe irked Scott more than the wrestling match, and then, suddenly—

His good feelings were gone. Somehow, they'd turned out to be as fragile as soap bubbles.

Scott felt his scowl returning, etching itself deeper than ever into his face. Jennifer withdrew her hand. It was quiet in the car until Scott steered into a parking space just outside of the old Ruby's Place. The red neon glowed against the night sky, casting Christmas-colored shadows across the snowdrifts.

"No one's here," Jennifer sighed, nervously tugging at her scarf. She leaned forward to look first one way and then the other. "Shouldn't everyone be here by now?"

"Maybe she's not open yet," Scott said. As though to prove his point, he turned his wrist to expose his watch. But the face grimaced at him. That was just the way it looked. The hands were pointed in such a way that it mimicked the appearance of a mouth pointed into a downward "V." It, too, knew the hour it displayed was dangerously late.

"I had always assumed it would take some time to warm up…no one ever likes to be the first person at the party…" Scott blubbered.

Jennifer made a face not unlike the one on Scott's wrist. "*I* assumed they'd have all been lined up at that door for an hour by now. I would have thought—based on the way you always talked about the place—that everyone would have had fond memories. The kind of fond memories that would have made it impossible to stay away. A place that makes you feel as good as you say this one did—a place that to this very day echoes through your heart…Now, don't roll your eyes at me, Scott Drummond. It does, I know you. I can tell. That funny little smile you always get when you talk about this place. And your father. It's all so vivid to you. Your dad is never far away when you remember it. Any other time, the stories you tell me about Walter, they're sort of…I don't know. Almost rote.

Like something the kids had to memorize for school."

"Ouch," Scott muttered.

"It's just that they're stories you've told so many times, they're kind of thin in spots. Like that nasty old Harley-Davidson shirt of yours," she teased.

"That's *your* Harley-Davidson shirt," Scott corrected, playing along. It was a long-running joke between the two of them, this ancient old motorcycle T-shirt that just kept following them along in their lives, first apartment to apartment and then house to house. Neither one of them wanted to lay claim to it, with the fraying neckline and the cracked screen-printing and the formerly-black material their various washing machines had turned gray. It was such an out-of-character item for either of them. And though they both tried to pretend they had no idea of its true origin, Scott knew it had belonged to one of Jennifer's old boyfriends.

It only bothered him occasionally that she still had it. Mostly, the *occasionally* occurred during those times when Jennifer seemed distant and tired and full of daydreams. But when she was with him, really with him—planning for a birthday party or a vacation, or sitting on the edge of their bed painting her toenails and laughing through some winding story of her day until she snorted—then he didn't mind the T-shirt at all.

She was a bit of a sentimental softie. That was all. Far more than Scott was. Maybe that was why she'd liked his stories of Ruby's.

Maybe that was why she was here now.

Why wasn't anyone else? Was Jennifer the last sentimental softie in town? Had the world really grown colder than December? Did no one ever keep a special place in their hearts anymore for the things that had meant something? Did no one else cling to a silly thing like an old T-shirt simply because it was connected to that something-special? Was everything disposable, even memories?

Again, Scott turned his eyes to the front of the old supper club. "Angela had so many problems getting that renovation completed on time," he said. "She really had to work at it to get that neon sign back up. Restoration was almost absurdly pricey. But that sign was so iconic. Probably the most important part of getting the place back exactly the way it was. Maybe even more important than that big old bar."

"I know," Jennifer murmured.

"And there was this weird accident with the pipes," Scott went on. "Just a few days ago."

"Right."

"So many people came out again to help clean it up."

"Yes. They did."

"And now what? A little snow keeps everyone away?"

"Surely not," Jennifer said. "Let's give it a little time. Christmas Eve means family's in from out of town, and it takes longer to get out of the house."

"Maybe everyone's already inside," Alessandra suggested, poking her head into the space between the front seats.

Scott and Jennifer both glanced at her with surprise. It was an odd feeling when your child—who had, what felt like a mere moment and a half ago, no ability to speak or even feed herself—started talking sense. A little like seeing the family dog put on a tie one bright sunny morning, walk down the stairs on two legs, and grab a briefcase before heading out the door.

"It's possible," Jennifer conceded.

"But where are the cars?" Scott asked. "The parking lots and the streets are totally empty." He pointed out the recently-plowed roadway, the lots surrounded by mounds of pushed-aside snow. Electric signs glowed from the front of The Page Turner bookstore and the diner and the It Ain't Over Yet flea market. But so did the letters beneath the businesses' names that proclaimed the stores were all closed. Strings of white lights twinkled for no admirers. Aluminum snowflakes groaned and screeched as they were tugged and pushed by the wind. Those tied on loosely clanged against the light poles, filling the air with an uneven hollow beat.

Jennifer squinted, leaning still closer to the windshield. So close this time, her breath drew mist on the glass.

"Are the lights even on inside?" she asked.

"Inside Ruby's?" Scott asked, doing some squinting of his own. "I'm not sure. They might not be."

Scott unclicked his seat belt. "Stay here," he told everyone. "I need to talk to Angela. Make sure everything's okay."

7.

RIAN STUMBLED ACROSS the front walk to the ancient Victorian home, trying to block the floodlight (where could it
have possibly come from?) with his hands. But it was no use.
That floodlight attacked his eyes with everything it had. He
cringed, sure he was feeling the beams through his eyelids.

"You! What're you doing out here snooping around?"
an older voice demanded. "On Christmas Eve, no less. You
think no one's watching tonight? Too busy? Well, think again."

He snapped the light off. Thankfully. But Brian was
still blinded in the aftermath. He blinked and rubbed at his
eyes as yellow spots continued to obscure anything in front of
him. "I—was looking—a hotel—bed and breakfast…"

The aged voice barked, "Nothing like that in town.
Gotta get on the highway for that kind of thing."

"So I—so I was beginning to realize," Brian stuttered,
squeezing his eyes shut as hard as possible in an attempt to
recover.

"You don't have family you're staying with?"

"No—I was here—to work. I'm a developer. For the
bank project."

"Ah, yes! The big teardown."

Brian felt a bit wounded that the town knew him in this way. The destructor. The eraser.

"Be nice to see the old thing replaced by something shiny."

"Will it?" Brian asked.

"Sure! Folks are always drawn to shiny things. It'll jumpstart redoing the downtown area. Bring it back to life."

Brian grunted, feeling certain this man was half of the older couple who had shown up at all of his public meetings. He had clearly memorized the talking points that Brian had spewed at those meetings. Probably, those points had been reinforced when he'd read the paper. Brian had been sure to repeat them to all the local reporters. It was simply his job—and it had clearly worked. But now, it pained him to think the message had permeated so deeply.

As his eyes adjusted, he was better able to make out the old man who had come outside to greet him. He was bald, with a mustache and glasses. In his robe and pajamas.

Once, Brian would have seen a chasm between the two of them. This night, though, he could only feel the scratch of his own wiry gray hairs around the backs of his ears and the weight of years that had managed to show him everything that he hadn't done yet. Why hadn't he chosen a life in which he could rescue instead of destroy? Why hadn't he been warned that once you get on a path as an adult there was little chance of getting off? That life's journey was far more escalator than an open woodsy field? Something you just had to ride until it deposited you at the end?

That was the way it felt, anyway.

"You must be cold," Brian said, noting the man's leather slippers. "I didn't mean to disturb you."

"Oh, I've got an agreement with the city," the man said. "They gave me the keys, even though I don't own the place. Kind of an unofficial caretaker of sorts."

"That's a lot to put on you."

"Easier than having to call authorities to shoo away all the folks that shouldn't be here. Besides, it's not without compensation."

So the city paid him. Was the property that much of a draw for problems?

"That many people try to get in?" Brian managed to ask out loud.

"The teenagers used to. Made it a regular den of in*eq*uity for a while."

"I think you mean iniquity."

"What's the difference?"

Brian barked a surprised laugh. "Not much, sometimes," he admitted.

"Did you really think this old thing could have been a bed and breakfast?" the man asked. "One that was *open?*"

Brian sighed. He liked this old man. Maybe it was because he was so protective of something that was falling apart. Finally. Someone cared.

"I sure would like a closer look at the place," Brian admitted. "You said you have the keys. Would you mind letting me take a peek inside?"

8.

SCOTT COULDN'T SEE A THING. Not through the hazy frost covering the front window of Ruby's. He tugged out his nearly-dead phone to text his wife, who was still waiting with the kids in the car. "Checking out back," he thumbed clumsily, not used to the tiny keyboard.

"Checking for what?" she asked, but instead of answering directly, he slipped the phone in his pocket and held up one finger in a *just a minute* gesture.

Scott rushed down the alley behind the old supper club. He raced past the staff-only entrances of the neighboring businesses and knocked at Ruby's. It was an ancient door, he noticed, with a tiny window. He took a step back to see if they were really there—the plugged-up holes along the bottom that some of the old-timers swore were bullet holes from the pre-Ruby speakeasy days.

"How about that?" Scott muttered, his fingers finding the indentions. They certainly could have been bullet holes.

But the old stories quickly drifted away from Scott, and he was flooded with all the sensations of those Christmas Eves at Ruby's Place. *His* Christmas Eves, the ones he'd lived himself. The proud feeling associated with wearing his first three-piece suit. The anticipation. The way the carols, sung in unison by the entire room, vibrated in his chest. Scott's past—while not entirely shiny—was not nearly as tarnished as it had been earlier that evening. Bittersweet fragments of his life swirled like bits of snow.

"Angela?" he croaked, reminding himself that this building did belong to her now. Funny—standing out here, it seemed that Ruby herself should be rushing to let him in.

When Angela didn't answer, he knocked again—more forcefully that time. Hard enough to make a clump of snow—filled with ice—tumble from the eaves.

The ice was both a rock and a fist; it struck Scott's head with a viciousness that sent him stumbling, struggling to get his feet steady beneath him. His hands cupped his head, tilted now toward the ground. The skin along his hairline and down his forehead stung and his entire skull throbbed in time with his pulse.

The pain just kept ringing, a bell that refused to stop echoing inside him. It was so strong, in fact, that Scott didn't even mind when he felt a hand on his shoulder. He needed help, and somehow, he felt certain that whoever was in possession of that hand could provide it. He followed wherever that still-unseen person wanted to lead. He was dizzy enough to feel like a regular cartoon character at that moment, with stars making circles around his head.

He was being led into a building. It was dark inside, maybe. Scott still couldn't be sure. His eyes were hardly open. But the warmth was welcome.

"Here," someone was telling him, peeling his hands away. "Hold this against your head."

"Is this ice?" Scott asked, feeling cold lumps through

a thin sheet of fabric. It seemed to him like an old-fashioned handkerchief, the kind his father had always carried. He laughed to himself. "Isn't ice what caused the problem in the first place?"

"Just sit down for a minute. Catch your breath and get your wits back about you," the same man's voice told him. "Here," he insisted, directing Scott with both hands. "Right here."

Scott propped himself onto a stool. He rested one of his arms on a countertop of some sort. No—wait—it had some sort of padding along the edge, as though it was expected that he would lean against it long enough to want a cushion. He was sitting at a bar.

A rather ornate, carved bar, it seemed as he pulled the ice away and blinked himself from the pain enough to get a good look for the first time. The darkness that obscured most of the room was interrupted, here and there, by a few trails of glittering light. Tables had been draped with linen and decorated with tea candles. He could make out the faint outline of a piano in the back corner.

"Ruby's Place," Scott murmured, placing the handkerchief full of ice on the bar.

"Don't act surprised," the man said. "You were banging on the door like you knew exactly what this place was. Demanding to be let in."

"I did—I mean—I was looking for Angela. But now that I'm here, it's just—exactly the way it used to be when I was a kid."

Scott inhaled deeply. "That smell," he said, "that's not—it's not marshmallows, is it?"

"Wouldn't be Ruby's Place on Christmas Eve without homemade toasted marshmallows and cocoa," the man said, reaching through a pocket of darkness to retrieve a teacup. It jiggled on a saucer as the man dragged it across the bar, coming to a stop right in front of Scott.

"It can't be," Scott said.

"Ruby's own recipe."

Scott tugged the cup closer and brought it to his lips. As soon as the sweetness of the cocoa and the gooey marshmallows hit his tongue, he felt it—finally. That old, familiar Christmas spirit that had been missing all season. It exploded through his chest, even as the cocoa scorched his mouth.

"It's so good to be back," Scott sighed. "Me and my dad, we came all the time."

"Every Christmas Eve," the man agreed from the barstool beside him.

"How would you know that?" Scott started, just before noticing the squat crystal glass sitting on a napkin in front of him.

"Scotch neat. That's what my father used to drink," Scott blurted as the man leaned forward—into the light—to grasp the glass.

The man's hand was familiar—as was the narrow gold ring he wore. Scott turned to look into the pair of blue eyes that had watched over him as a boy. And that grin he hadn't seen in decades, the same that had always been ready to forgive his childish indiscretions.

It couldn't be.

But it was.

Walter Drummond, who had not been alive to share a Christmas Eve with his son for twenty-six years, now put a hand on his son's shoulder. It was, Scott knew at that moment, the same hand that had guided him from the alley into the building.

With his other hand, Walter pushed some sort of wooden trinket box across the bar, toward Scott.

"It's so good to see you, son," Walter said. "But we don't have a lot of time. I have a story for you. And when I'm done, I'm going to need a little bit of help from you."

9.

DECEMBER 8, 1938

IT WAS A TERRIBLE THING to die so close to Christmas. Or so ten-year-old Walter thought as he paused to stare up at the now-vacant old Bonwit mansion.

It was especially terrible when the recently-deceased had to part from such a Christmas card of a house, a towering Victorian with turrets and gingerbread trim, the oldest in the entire city of Sullivan. And it was also especially terrible when, after a particularly snowy December, the house was surrounded by picturesque pine tree branches and dark wrought iron fencing, both of which were dotted with artistic white dobs.

The Victorian Mrs. Hetty Bonwit had lived in, right up until that very last breath, oozed holiday contentment. Even heaven couldn't have been a better place to wake up on Christmas morning. The only thing the old Bonwit home was missing were footsteps in the snow going up the front walk. Tracks to the front door always made a place feel homey on

Christmas.

But then again, Walter reminded himself as he stared up at the front door, the Bonwit place never did have tracks on the front walk. Around it, sure. But never up to the front door. The people of Sullivan would never head that way.

"Good riddance," Petey Collins growled.

Petey Collins, Walter's best friend since shortly after birth, shook his head at the empty house. For some reason, he had been especially brutal regarding the death of old Mrs. Bonwit. In fact, anytime the subject of Mrs. Bonwit had bubbled up in the last few days, Petey had turned the kind of cold that burned the skin if you held on to it too long. Far colder even than the wrought iron fence he and Walter now freely leaned on, no fear anymore of being attacked by an infuriated Mrs. Bonwit.

Petey's father ran the Sullivan Funeral Home in the same Collins family house where Petey and his younger sister had always lived. Lately, Petey had begun to adopt a kind of over-exaggerated bravery on the subject of death. Before that day, it had made Walter laugh to himself. All that put-on smugness. Petey's so-called tough exterior, Walter knew, really was just as soft as the graphite inside their school pencils.

But Petey's attitude on Mrs. Bonwit's passing jabbed like a toothpick at Walter's soft pink spots. This was getting out of hand. Walter couldn't dismiss it as mere big-talk anymore.

"Somebody's dead. Their whole life is over," Walter murmured, soft enough to reveal he regretted speaking up even as he formed the words. Almost as if he feared what Petey would do if he heard him. Twist the words and use them to make fun of Walter, surely.

Walter shifted his weight back and forth, waiting for

Petey's response. It was twilight, and the voices of mothers were bouncing down the street. Boys were being called home to dinner plates full of mashed potatoes. Bicycle wheels were spinning away.

"Yeah," Petey grumbled, draping his arms over the fence. He tried to hide a grimace as the wrought iron posts poked up into his armpits. "Somebody died, all right. But why should I care about *this* one? What did she do other than torture us? Stuck her face in that front window of hers, pounded on the glass and screeched at us, all she ever did." He jabbed at the air with his woolen glove, pointing at the old mansion. "Just waiting for us to get close enough so she could come after us, yell at us for daring to set foot on her property."

That was true enough. The ancient Bonwit house, with its enormous front porch that *should* have been welcoming, stood directly between Walter's neighborhood and the public library. The shortest route between the home of any child on Walter's street and the pair of giant stone lions, perpetually frozen into silent roars on either side of the library entrance, was through Mrs. Bonwit's yard.

Surely, any other woman would have smiled and waved at the children racing by. Maybe even invited them up to her porch in the warmer months, given them a glass of lemonade.

Mrs. Bonwit, though? As soon as a child would dare to tiptoe through the off-road course, the front door would bang open, and Bonwit would emerge, her back hunched, holding her cat to her chest, shouting random threats and waving her free arm to shoo them away.

Once, she'd come after Walter with a broom. Swinging it through the air like Lou Gehrig aiming for a fastball.

Walter had hated the way she treated him. Who wouldn't? The horrible part was, though, it went on so long, he stopped hating the treatment and started hating *her*. It was just that simple. And that natural. Walter was a good boy, after all. The sort to never flirt with trouble. The sort that turned his assignments in on time and shoveled the snow from his front walk without being asked. It always shook him to be accused, so angrily, of trespassing.

"Trespassing's the last thing it is," Walter's mother had assured him. "That strip out there between the houses, that's a city easement. It doesn't belong to anybody. You're doing nothing wrong."

But what his mother had said wasn't to make him feel better. It wasn't meant to soothe his scraped-raw pride. It was said harshly, one eyebrow raised in a *you'd better follow these instructions to a T* kind of manner. Walter was to get himself to the library and be back in time for supper. No excuses. Which meant he'd better make use of that shortcut, no arguments about it. His dad worked hard—and came home hungry. He shouldn't have to wait on Walter's long way around.

And so Walter continued to cut through, and Mrs. Bonwit continued to scream at him. When he had been certain she was back in her house—or had at least turned her back on him—Walter would whip around and stick his tongue out. To be accused of something you were not guilty of (a public easement, his mother had said! Didn't belong to a person but the city!), well, that could harden a ten-year-old heart faster than old man Pendleton's pond could freeze in the winter.

Walter, of course, wasn't alone. The rest of the children (surely made brave by similar pronouncements from their own parents) had continued taking the shortcut—most of them trampling angrily, not bothering to watch out for Mrs. Bonwit's daffodils or her mums. They didn't care if it somehow hurt Mrs. Bonwit's feelings, if it made her feel unheard or weak or unimportant, if it made it seem like they thought she was some old biddy. She had treated *them* like hooligans. It had simply been necessary to even the score.

And yet, now, Walter felt some remorse. Or guilt. Or maybe, for the first time in his life, the clock had simply run out on a problem before it had ever had a chance to get resolved. There was a shock in that, and a sharp pain that hit his chest when he inhaled too deeply.

"Think my old man's already gotten the bat drained?" Petey asked with a malicious grin.

Walter looked at him in horror, his mouth agape. A long stream of disgusted steam spilled out from between his twisted lips, forming a winter cloud between them.

"Come on," Petey said. "Don't pretend there was anything good about her. Look at that thing!" He pointed to a railroad tie at the edge of her front walk, the one with the sharp ends of nails poking out of it, meant to pop the bicycle tires of anyone getting too close.

"I don't know. Maybe we missed something.

"*Missed* something?" Petey repeated. He tugged off a glove to flick the cigarette he shouldn't have been smoking. "I won't miss her. Feel bad that my old man has to deal with her—*remains*." He grimaced.

Walter felt a sickness in him, the very first hint of an uncomfortable suspicion that the world might be, at its core, far too gruesome for a tenderheart like himself.

Maybe Petey was lucky that he had grown up in a bedroom only two floors over the truth of it all: the one and only funeral home in Sullivan. The end of the line for everyone in town. He didn't have to learn about the things you couldn't take with you. He'd already seen it every day. Dust to dust and all that.

Petey's father had embalmed everyone—the grand-mothers and the stillborn. He'd stared into the mangled faces of railroad accidents and victims of robberies gone wrong. Even into the blue-tinged face of the young man (who had, by all accounts, just fallen in love for the first time, and was off to meet his sweetheart beneath the moonlight) who'd trag-ically fallen through the ice of the usually rock-solid Pendle-ton pond, drowning before rescue could arrive.

Yes, Petey's dad had looked every tragedy that had be-fallen Sullivan right in the lifeless eye.

But Petey was wrong to imply that it had somehow not bothered him. Walter had once spied Mr. Collins from a distance, sitting on the back step of the funeral parlor, his head in his hands, crying.

Petey was also wrong to think that Mrs. Bonwit—by all definitions an old woman who had kept herself holed up in her Victorian home and demanded only that the town of Sullivan stay as far away as humanly possible—would not be any bother to his father.

The truth was, Walter suspected, Mr. Collins's job al-ways got to him.

Walter watched as Petey continued to puff away at his cigarette, exhaling toward the Victorian house in a way that suggested he'd blow smoke straight into the mean old lady's face, given the chance.

At least, that was how Walter read his friend.

The late afternoon sun glared at them, bouncing off the snow and forcing them to narrow their eyes into slits. The knit band of Walter's stocking cap turned his forehead sweaty and itchy. He rubbed at the hat band, saying, "I feel bad. I do. I can't help it."

Petey puffed his cigarette and scoffed. "Why don't you go to the bat's funeral, then?" he mocked.

In the distance, yet another woman's voice swirled through the winter air. A more familiar voice, this time.

Petey flinched, instantly flicking his cigarette into the snow where it hissed to its death. He popped a piece of peppermint candy into his mouth.

Sure. Big brave guy, Walter thought. Scared of a petite little woman, barely 4'4", in an apron with strawberries embroidered all over it. His mother, calling him to dinner.

She only had to call once. And there Petey went, jogging away down the street.

Walter stared up at the towering Victorian home, his friend's words lingering in the air like frozen fog.

Go to the funeral. It wasn't a bad idea. Maybe, Walter thought, it might soothe the ache in his chest, the lingering doubt about how he had treated Mrs. Bonwit. Now that it was all over, it occurred to him that maybe she would have been nicer if someone had extended a hand in kindness. Then again, maybe people like Bonwit always seemed not-quite-so-bad in the past tense.

Regardless, Walter could have been more considerate. They all could have. A late apology, he hoped, was better than none.

10.

DECEMBER 24, 2018

"WHAT DO YOU WANT IN THERE FOR?" the old man asked.

"I can't quite explain it," Brian admitted. He tilted his head back, looking up at the gingerbread trim that seemed to glow in the moonlight. "I almost feel, standing here, like there's magic in the place still."

The old man wheezed a laugh. "Magic? Not in this place. Never was. I can still remember being shooed away from it when I was a kid."

"Shooed away," Brian repeated.

"Sure. Old lady lived here. At least, that's how I thought of her when I was a kid. Funny—I'm far older now than she was then. You know I'm ninety?"

"You can't be," Brian said, and meant it.

"I am, at that. Bet I've got, oh, thirty years or so on Hetty Bonwit. Boy, she seemed ancient, though. Back when I still was so young I could count my age on my fingers. I used to think she had to be older than this very town. And *mean*—" The man drew the word out, singsong. "Meanest thing I ever did see. Used to chase everybody away, like I said. Now I'm the one doing the chasing. Funny, huh?"

"I'm sure the neighborhood appreciates you doing your civic duty," Brian said, relying on the kind of compliments that had helped him convince similar men in other states to let him tear down their town's monuments. "Mr.—" Brian raised his eyebrow, asking the man to fill in the blank while he extended his hand.

"Collins," he finished, tucking his enormous, blinding (and now, thankfully, dark) flashlight under his arm. "Peter."

"Peter," Brian repeated, shaking the man's hand. "You grew up in the area, then?"

The man nodded. "The original family home's walking distance from here. Sister lives there with her family now."

"We never do get too far from the places that have a hold on our heart," Brian said, nodding his understanding.

"Well, I don't know if it's truly as sentimental as that. I married, needed a home. The one next door to this place was for sale."

Brian offered a slight smile in his much-practiced understanding way. "But your adult house became *your* home. In a way that your childhood house never really was."

"Of course it did. Raised my own kids in the same house I'm in now, you know. Got far more years and more history in the house I've got now."

"Decades and decades," Brian agreed. "And *this* house," he said, patting the porch railing, "has seen plenty of phases, I'd assume."

"No—it hasn't! That's just it. This old place has been empty since the Bonwit woman died. Can you imagine? Since

1938!"

"How can that be? Not a soul has wanted it?"

"Oh, they've wanted it. You know. Non-locals come sniffin' around. Or maybe one of these younger couples come by who didn't know Bonwit personally. There's been interest. But it's always fallen through. Weird how that happens in this town. Something similar went on over at Ruby's Place. That business has been empty decades, too. Anyway, somewhere along the way, someone over at City Hall decided it would be best to put the old Bonwit house on the historic register. So now it can't even be demolished." He shook his head, disgusted.

"What's it like inside?"

"Gotta be a mess," Peter said. "As long as it's been empty. And as many times as the ne'er do wells have been chased away."

"Gotta be? When's the last time you were inside?"

Peter snorted at the ridiculousness of this question. For a second, Brian thought he could see the young Collins boy in his face, illuminated by the bluish glow of the Christmas moon. That snort had a *stop pulling my leg* ring to it. "I've *never* been inside," he admitted.

"Never?" Brian asked. "And you have the keys?"

"I'm no superstitious man," Peter told him. "Usually. But when it's about this Bonwit place—" His voice trailed as he shook his head. "I don't know. I get the chills anytime I get close to the door. Even now, all these years later, I expect the old lady's ghost to come swooping down the stairs, screeching at me for trespassing."

Brian offered a half-grin. "I *am* a developer," he reminded Peter. Actually, he only worked for a developer, but he didn't think that detail would help his case any.

"You don't mean to tell me you still want inside," Peter said. "Not after everything I told you."

"I'm sure you would like, for once in your life, to not live next to an abandoned property. To not have to keep watch on it. To forget the worries you've carried all these years."

"You know what a money pit this must be?" Peter asked, wagging a thumb at the entrance.

"Nope. I don't. That's why I think you should unlock the door and we should take a look," Brian said. He was careful to use the word *we* and not *I*. "Come on," he said, nudging Peter. "I bet you're dying to see it. Finally. After all this time. I'd be giving you the perfect excuse." *And you wouldn't have to go in alone*, he could have added, but didn't. He hoped the *we* part did that without having to spell it out, embarrassing Peter with the fact that he'd been too chicken to see it by himself. That his bravery extended only to shouts and flashlights.

"Come on," Brian said, taking a step for the door. "Let's do it."

Peter's eyes sparkled once more with boyish playfulness. And he rattled the keys from the pocket of his robe.

11.

DECEMBER 10, 1938

WALTER FOUND HIMSELF oddly unnerved standing just inside the entrance of the Collins home. He snatched his hat from his head and his nervous fingers kneaded the brim as he wondered why he could be bothered so thoroughly. Too afraid, even, to eat breakfast that morning. How many times had he knocked on Petey's door? Lingered on his front steps in the summer, waiting only semi-patiently for him to retrieve the baseball bat or roller skates he'd forgotten? Leaned his elbows on the second-story bedroom windowsill as Petey blew his cigarette smoke outside?

The truth, Walter slowly began to realize, was that he had spent most of their friendship avoiding all signs of the funeral portion of the home. He had most frequently entered through the back door, the one that led directly to the kitchen. He had clung to the staircase, eyes zeroed on the placement of his feet on the steps, to keep from accidentally glancing through the wooden sliding doors to the parlor. He had even, at times, held his breath as he darted toward Petey's room, in order to avoid the heavy smell of lilies hanging in the air. The smell of lilies, Walter knew, was the smell of death.

Those times he'd used the front door, the front porch? Why, those had been the days without a single car parked in the street outside. Days when Walter was certain no funeral was scheduled to take place, and he would find no coffin in the parlor directly beneath Petey's sister's bedroom.

There hadn't been any cars outside as Walter had hurried across the Collinses' snow-dusted lawn. Not that it mattered. He knew for a fact that a funeral was taking place that day. Petey was off somewhere else, living up his Saturday like normal. Petey's sister was surely with her own hopscotching friends. Their mother was somewhere in the living portion of the house, doing whatever her normal Saturday chores were. And there stood Walter, acting like a total stranger. Acting as though he wasn't sure he was welcome. He shifted his weight back and forth, trying to get up the nerve to head toward the parlor with the rows of folding chairs and the flowers and the shiny walnut casket with the gold handles.

The smell of lilies was especially thick that day.

From where he stood, Walter was at the perfect angle to glance through the open parlor doorway and see that the casket was open, the purple satin lining catching the overhead lights. The tip of Mrs. Bonwit's nose and a single white curl of hair—almost like a tiny white branch of a birch tree—stuck out from the edge of the casket.

Somber music droned on in the background. Nothing like the bright, bell-filled carols that filled the air above downtown Sullivan. Every December, it often seemed to Walter there were no longer any clouds in the sky above the town, only giant lovely billows of chords. The kind that made any landscape all the more picturesque.

These tones, though—they were cold. They dripped into Walter, bounced down his spine.

Walter began to sweat. Did death ever become something natural? To the elderly who had lost loved ones so many times? To the doctors who had seen it come for their patients? Did it ever truly seem like a part of life? Or did everyone—no matter how many times they looked it square in the glassy eyes—continue to greet death with that dark pit in the belly?

This was a bad idea. Walter didn't want to do this. He didn't want to see Mrs. Bonwit dead. He had just swiveled on his heel and lunged for the door when a tentative voice called, "Walter? Is that you?"

Walter gulped, his Adam's apple bobbing like an awkward character's in a comic strip. He felt every bit as ridiculous.

When he turned, he found himself looking directly into Mr. Collins's face. The same face he'd once seen twisted in pain, writhing on the back step of that very building.

This time, Mr. Collins's face was twisted with confusion.

"Are you—did you come—for Petey? He's not around, you know, he shot out of here early this morning." Mr. Collins wasn't indicating this was any great escape on Petey's part— *Petey* wasn't trying to skip out on Mrs. Bonwit's funeral. He wasn't afraid like Walter was. It was simply what Petey did on a Saturday morning. He lit out of there, as Mr. Collins was always saying.

His eyes kept bouncing over Walter's suit, the lapels peeking out from between the front folds of his topcoat.

Walter liked suits. He liked feeling grown-up, even if it

was only a sensation that accompanied a smartly folded pocket square and had nothing to do with any accomplishments or true rites of passage.

But not even his smart suit could make him feel grown-up that day. Standing there, in front of Petey's dad, Walter felt like a fool—the most common feeling of childhood.

"I—I—" Walter stuttered. He what? Nothing made sense. Why weren't there more people? Someone to distract from the fact that he'd shown up?

Walter's face bloomed like a giant pink peony. The kind that opened up in the town cemetery just in time for Decoration Day.

"Are you here for Mrs. Bonwit?" Petey's dad asked. But that expression on his face…he wasn't shocked. He was relieved. He was grateful that Walter had shown up. Walter offered a proud smile. Because this—the happy feeling of being relied on—made him feel grown-up. For more than any piece of clothing ever could.

"Come in, come in," Petey's dad said, resting a hand on Walter's shoulder. "This way to the parlor."

Walter allowed Mr. Collins to lead him toward a seat in the front row. Why was no one else seated yet? Where were the other mourners? Where was Bonwit's family?

Walter told himself he was surely just the first. Others were filing in behind him. He couldn't see them, not from his place in the front.

He knew that was wrong, though, the moment he saw the minister's face. The jerky hitch as he stepped up to the podium said he wasn't sure if he should even go through with the service. What would be the point, when the only person present was a ten-year-old boy?

The two—Walter and the minister—fidgeted nervously, staring at each other wide-eyed.

The minister nodded, finally, and a book was opened, though Walter couldn't be sure which one. Did Mrs. Bonwit deserve Bible passages? *Was* she as genuinely rotten as the rest of the town believed? Black and slimy pumpkins left on porches halfway through November had more appeal—or so it could have been successfully argued. Pumpkins didn't chase you away from the house screaming and swinging a broom.

Mrs. Bonwit didn't like children. She didn't like puppies and she didn't like the mailman. She didn't like Christmas carolers or invitations to tea from the Sullivan Historical Society.

She probably wouldn't have liked Walter coming to her funeral, either. Why would she? Walter stared at the casket, expecting the ghost of Mrs. Bonwit to rise, shake her fist, and chase him from the parlor. "Out!" she'd scream. And then she'd reach into her casket and pull out a broom. Maybe even send her cat to scratch his eyes out.

Wait. Was that what she had shouted at him? *Out?* Or had it been something different? Had he never listened to her, not once? Then again, why would anyone ducking a broom stop to fully understand a person? Who wanted to spend time with a rotten pumpkin?

"Mr.—?"

Walter realized the minister was speaking to him. It was, it seemed to him, the first time an adult had used the word *mister* to address him. "Drummond," he squeaked.

"A few words, perhaps."

"Yes," Walter said, assuming the minister was simply telling him he was going to go through with it, give the same sermon he usually preached at a funeral.

They stared at each other, both of them wordlessly

pleading for the other to hurry up and get this thing over with.

"I meant do *you* have anything to say, son."

"Oh." Walter slumped. "She—"

"Yes. Go on. Something from your heart."

"She…was my neighbor."

The minister seemed disappointed. "That's what's in your heart," he grumbled.

Walter thought. "Yes," he said simply. "That's it."

"Well," the minister announced. "It is a fine thing to be. A neighbor. And a reminder to us all that this is what we are to each other, above all else."

And then it was over, the whole thing, in all of its awkwardness. There she lay: Mrs. Bonwit, her nose and her single white curl and her hands folded on her chest.

Walter had to get out of there. Race home and tear off his suit, hang it back in his closet before anyone at home could see him in it. There was no question about it now. This was a mistake.

At the exit, Petey's dad pressed his hand against Walter's chest. "Don't leave before signing the guest book," he said.

Walter didn't want to sign any guest book. He didn't want anyone to know he'd been there. It felt shameful, somehow, being the only one. Like everyone else in the town of Sullivan was smart enough not to lose sight of the truth of Mrs. Bonwit, not to forget the depths of her horribleness. They were right not to come. Of course they were. There was a rightness in numbers, Walter had often thought. There had to be. Everyone else knew that forgiveness that came simply because a person had died was hollow. Why hadn't he seen it himself?

If Mrs. Bonwit could have risen out of that casket, she would have screamed against the notion of being forgiven by Walter. She would have popped the tires of Walter's forgiveness, tossed it into the closest mud puddle.

Yes, Walter was the one and only fool in the entire town of Sullivan. Why would he want a record of his foolishness? A document of it?

He could not sign that guest book.

"I really should be going," he started. "My mother—" even though it was still hours from dinner, and his mother didn't need him. For anything. Walter's mother was a giant workhorse of a woman, the sort who rarely needed anything ever. A firewood chopping, fuse fixing, wrench-wielding, car-repairing woman, without whom Walter's family would have stumbled along in life. Because Walter's father was just that—a stumbler. A man who had never, not once to Walter's recollection, ever fixed anything right. Walter had often thought his parents had gotten together because his father was so bad at everything that he would not mind being with a woman who could do everything. A man like Walter's father did not find it embarrassing, only a relief.

Petey's dad frowned at him. He knew Walter's mother. Why hadn't he said father? Petey's dad might have believed that Walter's father needed him.

"It was explicit," Petey's dad said. "In the instructions Mrs. Bonwit left. She wanted whoever showed up to the funeral to sign in." His eyes pleaded. Walter could not be sure why Mr. Collins felt this was so important. Maybe, as the funeral director, he had simply formed a habit of honoring last wishes, no matter what the wishes were and who they'd been wished by.

Petey's dad had his hand on Walter's shoulder again,

and he was leading him toward the guest book, propped open on an ornate brass stand inside the door. His grip wasn't exactly tight, but just firm enough that Walter would have to wrench himself away in order to break free. And if Walter did do that—if he fought against Mr. Collins and squirmed and bolted, wouldn't that make this whole funeral business look like something? Like it was somehow meaningful and important? Isn't that the last thing that Walter wanted? Wouldn't he prefer to be able to shrug and say, "I only felt a little sorry for the mean old bat"? Or maybe, "I never wanted to go there. I was on my way downtown, and I got shoved inside. Mean old trick that bunch of big kids played on me."

Yes, he wanted that.

He had no choice. Rather than argue with his best friend's father, he snatched up the pen and he scrawled his name. As he made the first loop of the "W," it struck him that he could make it sloppy. So sloppy that it was illegible. "Me? No, that wasn't me at all," Walter could lie, later on. "I wouldn't be seen at the witch's funeral." Of course not. He knew better. He wasn't stupid or too tenderhearted. No, he knew better. Just like the rest of the town.

Once he was finished with his purposefully sloppy scribble, he handed the pen back and smiled. He turned toward the door, racing for the exit before Petey's dad could do something awful, like invite him to stay for dinner, at which time he would remind his son he could be a more caring young man—like his friend Walter.

Walter headed home and he removed his suit. He put on his dungarees and his plaid coat and he raced outside, pretending he'd been out the entire day. He returned home for supper and he ate his workhorse mother's pot roast and he went to bed and he knew that no one would ever be the wiser.

Well, there was Mr. Collins, of course, but he wouldn't betray Walter. Not his own son's very best friend. He had surely known from looking at Walter how he had regretted showing up. How he'd only gone in as a favor to Mr. Collins, who had seemed so relieved that someone had shown up. Mr. Collins had himself once been a boy, and he knew that you didn't rat out someone who'd done you a favor *that* big.

No, Walter told himself, closing his eyes on this awful day, no one would ever know he'd gone to that dreadful Mrs. Bonwit's funeral.

Walter fell asleep smiling at the certainty.

That is, until five days later, when the summons arrived from Mrs. Bonwit's lawyer.

12.

December 24, 2018

The truth was, Gregory had been feeling exactly like Scott for the last month—that Christmas had lost its shimmer. He had assumed, as the days had trudged ever closer to Christmas, that it was only him. And then, for a brief moment, there had been something close to hope in knowing that someone else was dealing with the same thing. Maybe, Gregory'd thought for the tiniest blip of a moment, the two of them could raise each other's spirits inside Ruby's Place.

Now, though, as he looked up and down the dead street, he wondered about everyone else. Was everyone in the town of Sullivan suffering in silence? Were they really all going to sit this holiday out at home?

He unlocked the passenger-side door of his ancient Volvo, and stared at his suit, the same one he'd worn to his sister's wedding two weeks earlier. He'd picked it up from the cleaner's a week ago and had neglected to carry it inside his apartment. It had, in fact, been draped over the front passenger seat enough days in a row that he had begun to think he ought to just give it a name. *Chuck*, he'd thought at first, but that was all wrong. A suit needed a formal name. *Charles*. Maybe even *Charles I*.

But as he stared at Charles, his hope for a bright and shiny Christmas Eve faded completely and his sour feelings came back home. He wished with everything he had that he could find an excuse not to go to Ruby's Place.

All around him, for weeks on end, new beginnings had been unwinding their petals. Word in town had it that Rob and Geena, two Sullivan childhood sweethearts—the Jack and Diane who had, sometime in the late '80s, scrawled their names in a patch of wet sidewalk concrete not far from the entrance of Ruby's Place—had reunited. Tina had expanded the It Ain't Over Yet flea market. Tonight, Angela was reopening Ruby's Place. But Gregory? He hadn't had a single new beginning attached to his name in ages.

He was tired of fighting back pangs of jealousy. Even at his own sister's wedding. How was it that so many people could go out and just *find* new starts laying around everywhere? How was it they could see them so easily, pluck them like four-leaf clovers right out of the ground? Everywhere that Gregory looked, all around him, he only saw the same old three-leaf clovers. Over and over again. A whole sea of sameness.

Day after day after day, he undertook the same routine. One hour, one week, one month nearly indistinguishable from another.

It was, he'd once tried to tell himself, the worst part of adult life—the day-in, day-out of it all. But this argument was house-of-cards flimsy. Other people managed to break their routines all the time with new jobs and new spouses and new adventures, he'd remind himself. And the pangs would start in all over again.

He reminded himself that the reopening of Ruby's Place did offer a chance to break a few monotonies—the routine of his evenings at home and, even, the solitary ways of the past few holiday seasons.

But in his heart, it felt more like a backward step. Ruby's was a place he'd gone in his youth. Gregory didn't want to go backward. He needed a shiny new—something. He wanted bright wrapping paper and a big red bow and the unexpectedness of what lay in the box.

Maybe, he thought, he should get in his car and just start driving. Wherever the car ran dangerously low on gas, that's where he'd spend his holiday.

That would be kind of an adventure, wouldn't it? A forced one, perhaps, but wasn't it better than the other available options?

Still, the promise he'd made to Scott nagged at him. He'd told Scott he'd be there for the grand opening. It wasn't right to back out now.

Surely, he thought, he would feel better once he got there. But as soon as Gregory put his hand on the shoulder of Charles I, he knew that the cleaner's had gotten out the wine stain from the sleeve, but the suit was still somehow soiled with the down-in-the-dumps feeling that had permeated everything Gregory'd touched these past few weeks.

Which was another thing that had become quite monotonous. Still—

"A promise is a promise," he grumbled as he tugged the suit free.

He slammed the door and glanced up and down the

street. How many people in town had made a similar promise to Angela, assuring her they'd be at her opening? Where were *they* now?

"Am I the only guy left in the world that follows through?" he asked himself.

Gregory rattled the keys out of his coveralls as he made his way across the lot, back to the entrance. He'd change, make his appearance. He didn't have to stay all night, of course. As long as he made good on his word. A quick hello, a drink. Surely he could stomach that much.

That was when he noticed a light on. Pouring through a window from the basement of the Bank of Sullivan. One he definitely hadn't left on himself.

13.

DECEMBER 15, 1938

THE INCREDIBLY OFFICIAL-LOOKING LETTER arrived from the attorney's office addressed to Walter.

As soon as the postman pressed the envelope into Mrs. Drummond's hand, she growled and began that marching stomp of hers, the one that announced she meant business and quite often followed the declaration that she was about to give someone (usually someone she had deemed *a real piece of work*) a piece of her mind.

Walter had often wanted to warn her that if she wasn't careful, she might very well wind up giving away so many pieces, she'd find herself without a mind at all. But when she was on the rampage, her sense of humor was nowhere to be found. Probably on its way to catching the next bus out of town, which was where Walter usually wished he was when his mother was tearing into someone.

Her galoshes clomped down their front hall, depositing clods of wet, half-melted snow onto the tile. "Walter Edward Drummond," she boomed. Her face was especially ruddy, and judging by her tone, it was far less from the cold than it was from her annoyance with him.

"An attorney?" she asked while rattling the envelope. "So close to Christmas. What have you *done?*"

Walter, as he'd frequently been reminded, had been a constant source of ruined dates and get-togethers. Holidays especially. Chicken pox one Christmas. Mumps another. A sledding fiasco resulting in a broken leg less than two hours into what had promised to be an especially lovely Christmas morning. Still another Christmas Eve day spent trying to rescue a six-year-old Walter from the woods behind his grandparents' home, where he'd gotten completely turned around and confused by the sameness of snow-covered pines.

Walter was no daredevil. He was simply unlucky. This appeared to be yet another punch of bad luck.

"You've finally done it this time, have you?" she snapped, digging her thumb under the envelope's flap.

"Done what?" Walter asked. Petey was the dare-taker. The cigarette-sneaker. The one who *needed* to look over his shoulder to make sure no adult was watching. Walter had never done anything that required him to tiptoe or act in secret. Wrapping his bicycle around a tree or being surrounded by a loose pack of dogs was just another strike of his dumb luck.

Walter felt sick wondering what his rotten luck had gotten him into this time. And he wondered why bad luck pursued him so viciously, chasing him down his street, tackling him, throwing him headfirst into yet another snowbank.

Why didn't bad luck go after Petey every now and then? Now, there was a boy who was, as Walter's mother would say, *just asking for it.*

He watched his mother wrestle the letter from the envelope, her frown deepening as she read. When she finished, she dropped her arms by her sides and gave Walter a look he'd never seen cross her face before. At that moment, he wasn't sure how to decode it.

Later, he would imagine it was the same look the farmer gave his rotten dud of a goose just before it inexplicably laid that very first perfect golden egg.

The offices of Arthur K. Pulcheck, Esquire, advertised that the attorney who worked there was exactly the sort anyone would expect Mrs. Bonwit to hire. Which is to say—cheap. Located in the basement of the Bank of Sullivan, the office was damp and poorly lit. It contained furniture so badly scuffed, Walter wondered if Mr. Pulcheck was actually the representative of a pack of coyotes with especially sharp toenails.

Then again, maybe he got his decorating inspiration at the dump.

Come to think of it, the longer Walter stood in the doorway, the more he felt convinced he was detecting the faint smell of something rotting. Not a bad smell, like garbage. More like the musty, earthy smell of decaying autumn leaves.

"Mr. and Mrs. Drummond," Mr. Pulcheck greeted, taking Walter's parents' hands in his own, one after another. He offered his idea of a smile, but the effort it took him to stretch his lips over his teeth turned the expression into more of a grimace. He smelled of strong aftershave and his jacket sleeves ended a good two inches above his wrists. He put such earnestness in the handshakes he offered Walter's parents that a greasy lock of black hair tumbled across his forehead.

Walter straightened himself, preparing for Mr. Pulcheck's greeting. Walter was terrible at introducing himself to adults. They were always expecting him to know how to shake their hands and then twisting their brows in disappointment with how he shook, bumping their fingers or squeezing too hard.

Mr. Pulcheck did not expect or even invite a handshake from Walter. The only sign that Mr. Pulcheck was acknowledging Walter's existence was the door he left slightly ajar, allowing that other—slightly smaller—Drummond to pass through.

All of it added up to the fact that Mr. Pulcheck assumed that Walter's father was the one he had summoned to his office. It was not an unreasonable assumption. Still, it irked Walter a bit, mostly because his parents were not attempting to correct him.

Walter wiped his brow. His heart beat at eighty miles an hour. He considered turning around and running back out the door. But where would he go? It was the problem of every ten-year-old. He was shackled to whatever it was that waited for him.

"What is this all about, Mr. Pulcheck?" Walter's mother asked. She sat straight and severe, in her Sunday clothes. Maybe she thought the smell of the church was bleeding off her too-small hat, the one she always wore to services, with the little red cherries and the gob of black mesh on it. Why, she was quite the pious one, her hat insisted. So unlike her rotten son.

Walter's mother was obviously still convinced that this was going to be bad news. It was probably the most traveled path a person's mind took when a vague letter arrived from an attorney—toward catastrophe. But it still stung. She was well aware of Walter's track record with bad luck, and she could have had a little sympathy for her only child.

Walter pouted, wondering, yet again, what it would take to finally send his bad luck packing. If life was starting out like this, where would he be when he was twenty? Thirty?

"One week ago," Mr. Pulcheck said, turning his eyes toward the file on his desk and his bald spot toward the Drummond family, "Walter attended Hetty Bonwit's funeral."

His mention of the funeral seemed to darken the office even more. And it was already quite dark all on its own. Every inch of the room—the desk, the walls, the floor, the shelves—were made of wood covered with a stain that was quite nearly black. To combat the dimness, Mr. Pulcheck had only a desk lamp that cast a sickly glow and the tiniest sliver of sunlight which filtered in through a crack in his window shade.

"He did?" Walter's mother looked at him with a mix of shock and dread. "You went to her funeral?"

Mr. Pulcheck twisted his neck back and forth, bouncing his gaze between Walter and his father. He frowned, his mind resetting itself as it became clear which one of them had been the true recipient of his letter.

"What were you doing at her funeral?" Walter's mother asked him, in a tone that said she knew she needed to ask—especially in front of an authority figure like Mr. Pulcheck. It proved she was a good mother. *Any* good mother would want to get to the bottom of this story, after all. But her tone also told Walter she was not looking forward to knowing the answer.

Walter blushed, unsure what to say. His scribbled signature hadn't done any good. And why would it? It was such a silly idea, he saw now. Petey's father had surely contacted Bonwit's attorney and provided Walter's name. But Walter also felt a surge of annoyance. How could Mr. Collins have done this—whatever *this* was—to Walter? How could he put him in this situation?

Walter's father squirmed in his chair, his son's awful luck and his wife's big mouth clearly making him dread whatever it was that was coming next.

"And according to the instructions left in her will," Mr. Pulcheck said, "his presence at the funeral means he is entitled to an inheritance."

His father stopped squirming. His mother leaned forward.

"Inheritance?" his mother repeated. "Walter?"

"Yes. According to this," Mr. Pulcheck said, pointing an ink-stained finger at the document on top of his desk, "the contents of Mrs. Bonwit's estate are to be divided among the attendees of the funeral."

Walter's father gulped. His mother startled. "Did you know?" she asked Walter.

All he could do was shake his head.

"How many people attended?" his mother asked, wiping the corner of her mouth. She was actually *salivating*.

Mr. Pulcheck straightened up, looking her square in the eye. "Counting your son?"

His mother nodded.

"Why—one," he answered.

Walter watched his mother's face flush and her chest heave.

"So he gets everything?" his father asked incredulously. "The entire estate?"

"Everything that's left, yes."

"Left?" his mother repeated.

"Yes," Mr. Pulcheck began, twisting a fountain pen between his fingers. "There were quite a few debts. Her husband had trouble a few years back—we've all had trouble, but Mr. Bonwit especially. It seems his financial woes were the reason behind his…" Mr. Pulcheck's voice trailed as he struggled to figure out how to phrase it tactfully. "…untimely demise," he finally finished. "His business went under. He left his wife in quite the dire straits. Many family antiques—and, really, nearly anything the couple had with value—had to be sold off. It was quite hard on Hetty. She felt the world had stolen from her. First her husband and then the things she'd loved so much."

"So the house was…empty?" Walter's mother asked.

"Well, now, it wasn't *completely* empty—she had some basic furniture, places to sit and sleep, that sort of thing. Some clothing. Some dishes to eat on. But the china and the silver and the Colonial furnishings?" Mr. Pulcheck shook his head.

"What was she so protective of?" Walter's mother wanted to know. "If she had nothing of value anymore? Why all the shooing away of the children?"

"The house was all she had left," Walter said quietly. "She was afraid of someone else coming up that walk to announce she didn't have a home anymore. That they were coming for that, too."

Walter's mother shot him a look. "Awfully presumptuous," she grumbled.

But Walter knew, in his heart, that he was right. And it made him feel even worse for all his days spent hating Mrs. Bonwit and bad-talking her. She'd been afraid. It was a terrible thing to think about her in that house, all alone, constantly fearful.

Walter slumped. He should have tried to be poor Mrs. Bonwit's friend.

"So—we—get the house?" Walter's father wanted to know.

"No, actually," Mr. Pulcheck said. "It was a somewhat unorthodox situation. Hetty Bonwit was quite beloved."

Walter's mother let out a short, sharp bark of disbelief. "Hetty *Bonwit*," she repeated.

"Why—yes." Mr. Pulcheck reached up to smooth his greasy hair back into place. "I know that in recent times, she's been somewhat of a—how should I put this?"

"Thorn in the sides of everyone in Sullivan?" Walter's mother finished.

Mr. Pulcheck flinched. "In her day, Hetty Bonwit was the sweetheart of Sullivan. From a prominent family. She won every beauty contest and was a draw to every parade in town when she was young. After she married, that home of hers was—well, it was almost a hotel."

"Hotel?" Walter's mother repeated.

"Well, because so many people came through there," Mr. Pulcheck said.

When Mrs. Drummond continued to stare at him as if he'd lost his mind, he explained, "That was the home where Hetty was a child. Her own family had made quite a bit of money in the railroad business, you see. When she married, her parents handed the keys—and the deed—to Hetty and her husband. But the place was so enormous, the elder couple had their own suite in the house. They—that is, Hetty's parents—lived out the rest of their days right there, in the same house with the Bonwits.

"Hetty's parents were never alone," Pulcheck went on, "and they were never without some new event to look forward

80

to. The home hosted all sorts of parties and gatherings during those years. And if you needed a place to stay—for whatever reason—you could bet you could find room at the Bonwits' place. Either in the gatehouse out back or in the house itself. And it was an open-ended invitation. You stayed as long as you needed. Yes," Pulcheck finished, "that house once had a very open door, indeed."

All three Drummonds stared back at Mr. Pulcheck in shock.

"I have a hard time believing that's the same person," Walter's mother admitted.

"Yes," Pulcheck said. "Well. I suppose her more recent behavior has—how shall I put it—*usurped* previous memories. And that's why no one else showed for Hetty's funeral. Not even the Sullivanites who are still in town who were themselves beneficiaries of the Bonwits' charity."

There's only so many times you can be chased away before you decide you're never going to attempt again, Walter thought.

"I just can't believe it," his mother blubbered. "I suppose—we're somewhat new to that neighborhood—rent went up at our old home, you see—" The truth was, the Drummonds had moved into their current home more than four years ago, and it had only been from a few blocks away. Walking distance. Closer to the Collinses' house, to Walter's delight.

When had this transformation occurred in Hetty, exactly? What was the date? Why had Walter's parents never— not once—heard music and laughter and voices coming from the old Victorian house? Hadn't they been close enough, even in the old house? What about the neighbors around Hetty? The Drummonds' minds spun as they tried to come up with a decent explanation.

Beside his quiet parents, Walter wondered: Had Mrs. Bonwit had friends? Real friends, like he and Petey were? Had she shooed them away, too? He could never imagine lashing out at Petey, no matter what horrible thing happened to him.

"To get back to your question of the house," Mr. Pulcheck said, picking up a few of the papers on his desk, "it appears that the bank owns it. *Has* owned it. Ever since Mr. Bonwit's death. But there was such affection for Hetty—"

"*Affection?*" Walter's mother broke in.

Mr. Pulcheck cleared his throat. "Well. Yes. There was such affection for Hetty, those in charge here at the Bank of Sullivan allowed her to live in it. The agreement was until her death. And now, what the bank will do with it remains something of an open-ended question."

"But the bank owns it," Walter's father repeated, just to be sure.

"Yes," Mr. Pulcheck agreed. "The bank owns it."

"So the antiques are gone," Walter's mother said. "And the jewelry and the silver. And the house is owned by the bank."

"Yes."

"I'm also assuming that Hetty's account here is—"

Mr. Pulcheck raised a hand and curled his thumb and fingers toward each other, forming a zero.

Now, Walter's mother was beginning to look as though the blood was draining from her face straight to the feet she'd crammed into her best black leather block heels.

"What's left, exactly?" Walter's father asked. "A cat and some house dresses?"

"The cat has been taken in by the family of an employee here at the bank," he apologized.

It struck Walter that Mr. Pulcheck was rather dusty, a

relic of a human, granted only the power in life to deal with remains. The tattered remnants. Which was all that Walter was getting.

His bad luck was striking all over again.

"*Mr.* Bonwit was the one who hired me," Mr. Pulcheck explained. "To manage his estate. Get his affairs in order. At the time, it seemed quite responsible. Now, looking back, it seems rather ominous. And, perhaps, somewhat obvious. I should have known that Mr. Bonwit was preparing for—well. For the end. I did not realize how bad things had gotten for him. Oh, I knew his financial situation. But I didn't know how hard he was taking it. The times have been a struggle for everyone. We've all suffered, each one of us facing our own tragedies."

"But why are we *here*, Mr. Pulcheck?" Mrs. Drummond growled. Walter feared she was about to give away yet another piece of her mind.

Mr. Pulcheck smiled. "There is one item that remains."

He paused, a smile on his face. No response came from Walter's parents.

"I suppose Mr. Bonwit's request would have proved somewhat complicated if a large group had attended the funeral," Mr. Pulcheck said. "But the task is simple, because Walter was the only person to sign the guest book."

He leaned to the side, throwing open his bottom desk drawer. "And so, this morning, I removed this from the vault. Which is where it's been ever since Mr. Bonwit left it with me."

He lifted up a single item and placed it on his desk. He moved in such a swift motion, Walter and his parents all gasped and leaned back, as though the item were something that could do real damage. A revolver, perhaps.

Walter's mother even placed a hand over her heart, as though to protect it from some blow.

Walter's father leaned forward, blocking Walter's line of vision. His parents' curiosity was not necessarily more important or more powerful than Walter's, only pushier. It surprised Walter, and it perplexed him, too.

Why was this thing not entirely his? Why were they extending their hands this way? Why were their mouths still watering? Where was Walter in all of this?

"That looks like—is it a—music box?" his mother asked.

"Yes!" Mr. Pulcheck exclaimed, seeming glad that the item was so easily recognized. "It was his business, you know. Mr. Bonwit. He made music boxes.

"I did happen to notice that the metal winder on the bottom is broken," Mr. Pulcheck said. "It's been twisted to the side, see here? I was afraid it might fall out, but it seems frozen in place. And even though it's broken, it's still quite lovely, don't you think?"

It was at that. Rosewood with brass filigree corners.

"A—*broken* music box?" Walter's mother asked.

"A music box no longer," Mr. Pulcheck corrected. "Mr. Bonwit disclosed that he had removed the mechanism and replaced it with something for Hetty. An insurance policy, of sorts. He told me—and here's what I *really* feel guilty about, what should have tipped me off that he had somewhat dark plans—that if anything were to happen to him, its contents would save Hetty. Should she ever find herself in *need* of a rescue, that is. He said what was in this box was important enough that if Hetty wound up never withdrawing it, the box needed to be bequeathed to someone else even after *her* passing. You see? Which is where we are now."

"What's in it?" Walter's mother demanded, the pendulum of her hopes swinging in the opposite direction yet again.

"I don't know, ma'am."

"You never *looked?*" she asked. "How could you never look?"

"It was not in my instructions to look. It was in my instructions specifically *not* to look."

"You always follow *instructions* that closely?" she asked, raising the corner of her lip in disbelief.

"I do, ma'am. In fact, that's why Mr. Bonwit hired me. He told me that he needed to bring these requests to a man he could trust."

"And you were that man," she finished.

"It does appear that way, yes. In fact, he told me I was the only honest attorney he'd ever met."

Walter's father laughed despite himself.

"If you are so inclined," Mr. Pulcheck said, his own curiosity on display, "I can open it for you now."

Walter's mother nodded eagerly.

Mr. Pulcheck twisted the brass latch and lifted the lid.

Again with the leaning, the gasping, the wide eyes. His mother reached forward and pulled something from the box. Walter had to crane his neck to see.

Money. It was money. His heart whacked and thudded. *How much?* he wondered as he watched his mother's fingers flip through the bills, counting.

"*Three dollars?*" she shrieked. "Is this some sort of joke?"

Mr. Pulcheck blinked up at her, expressionless. "Joke?" he repeated. He turned back down toward the papers splayed on his leather desk blotter. "No. Nothing in here indicates a joke."

Walter's mother clenched her jaw and dropped the dollars back into the box. In thirty seconds, she had won and lost a fortune. Cheeks growing ever pinker with frustration, she snarled, "Why in the world would a person go to such trouble over three lousy dollars?"

Mr. Pulcheck gulped and sifted through the items on his desk. "Well, there are some instructions here." He held up an envelope. The message across the bottom indicated, "To be opened in Hetty's time of need, or following her death."

"As you can see," Pulcheck said, turning the envelope over, "I have never broken the seal."

Walter's father leaned farther forward. "Go on, go on." As though still hoping that somehow, it might contain a map to a hidden fortune.

Pulcheck slid a silver letter opener under the flap and placed a pair of wire spectacles on his nose before reading. "Well," he said. "Well."

"What is it?" Walter's father asked. "What are we missing? There has to be something."

"These instructions are, uh, they are somewhat…unorthodox," Pulcheck said, flushing now with his own embarrassment.

"Yes?" his father pressed.

Mr. Pulcheck removed his spectacles. "Mr. Bonwit indicates the recipient of those dollars—whether Hetty or a funeral attendant—should treat the dollars as seeds."

Walter's mother sighed with an exasperation the depths of which Walter would never again hear, not in the length of his entire life.

"Seeds," she spat.

"Yes. Just as seeds are planted and grow into plants that produce many fruits that then produce more seeds—and on and on—these dollar bills can be planted, and many, many more dollars will be reaped in return."

"How does he—plant?" his father asked, gesturing toward the attorney with an empty open hand.

Walter's mother shook her head and pursed her lips.

Mr. Pulcheck smiled apologetically and said, "By giving the money away."

14.

DECEMBER 24, 2018

PETER UNLOCKED THE ENTRANCE to the Bonwit home, twisted the doorknob, and let it swing open.

He gestured in a *you first* way at the cracked-open doorway and took a step backward across the porch, closer to the railing.

"Should I be having second thoughts?" Brian asked. "Something you know about this place?"

Peter shuffled his feet. "I can't help it. It's just ingrained in me that I'm not supposed to be in there. Even after all this time."

"You don't believe the structure's unsound?"

"Oh, no, nothing like that. It was inspected again not all that long ago."

"Inspected?"

Peter shrugged. "The city does that every so often. Probably because it's their property now."

"Ever since Bonwit died?"

"Right."

"Why hasn't interest been strong enough for anyone to follow through with purchasing this place? A lovely old house like this?"

Peter hugged himself. "Sullivan's a small town, and not immune to gossip. What was the old party game? You remember—Telephone? Wasn't that it? Whisper the same secret into an ear, one after another, everyone at the party, and by the time you get to the end of the line, that last person hears something totally different than what the first person said?"

"Sounds like something the girls might have done at sleepovers," Brian said. He smiled at the old man, wanting him to join in on a shared roll of the eyes.

"It's the only way I can account for the wilder stories about this place," was all Peter could say.

"Such as?"

Peter tried to smooth his thin white hair over the crown of his head. "Such as Hetty's husband had somehow reached out from the grave to help her."

"Like he made provisions in his will?"

"Probably," Peter said. "Probably that's what everybody meant."

"Probably?" Brian repeated.

Peter let out a breathy, nervous chuckle and shook his head. "Gossip's a funny thing," he said. "It spreads and kind of hardens, you know? Becomes truth, after a certain point."

"I suppose," Brian said. "Any other wild tales about buildings in this town? The bank doesn't have some deep, dark secret, does it?"

"No, but Ruby's Place might."

"Oh, come on."

"I'm serious!" Petey insisted. "The way folks around here talked about the old Ruby's Place the last few years, you'd think it was flat-up cursed. Like anybody who ever thought about trying to set up shop in there was going to regret it. The place had all kinds of stuff wrong with it."

"I came from a meeting with Scott Drummond at the bank, and he talked about going there tonight with his family," Brian told him.

"I don't like to disparage anybody," Petey said, "but I wonder about Angela. About why she'd suddenly want to buy the place. She never seemed prone to harebrained ideas when she was a kid. Seemed more practical than that."

"You don't expect her to have a good opening night?"

"I dunno. I just think sometimes, buildings almost have a personality. Like they're alive or something. Maybe that sounds odd to you."

It didn't. Not at all. It was exactly the kind of thing that Brian had been thinking before pulling to a stop in front of the Bonwit place.

"Sometimes, I think I catch the tiniest hint of music," Peter said. "Funny, tinny sounding music. High-pitched."

"Coming from this place?" Brian asked.

"Mr. Bonwit owned a music box company," Peter said, his voice drifting off and becoming far away.

Brian wasn't sure if Peter had actually heard this music himself, or if the gossip of Sullivan, as he'd described, had somehow put this idea in his head.

But one thing was certain—Peter was not going to be the first one to take a step inside.

So Brian did. He made that first move.

He walked inside the old Bonwit house.

15.

INSIDE THE BANK, Gregory tossed his suit—still cloaked in dry cleaner plastic—onto the nearest teller counter.

"Hello?" he called out. "Anybody in here mean to leave a light on?"

No one called out in return.

"Scott?" he tried, his voice cracking. "You come back for something?"

Still nothing.

He glanced about at the spaces filled only by shadows. He tried chuckling to himself, admitting, "Been a long time since I've had a bad case of goosebumps." Scott *had* seemed in a bit of a rush to get out of the bank after they'd talked. Probably just forgot to turn a light off.

As sound as this reasoning was, it still didn't keep his feet from moving so cautiously across the lobby carpet that he was very nearly tiptoeing.

"Hello?" he called again. He strained, trying to make out a response.

A rustle. Coming from—the basement? Maybe? Gregory had never been in the basement. The space had been unused as long as he'd been an employee. It had never been deemed off-limits, exactly, but Gregory had been told there was no need to clean it.

Gregory had imagined a warehouse of sorts. A storage space for out-of-date records and old office equipment. Boxes filled with those ancient bank teller visors with the green face shields. Rows of dented old filing cabinets, maybe.

What greeted him on the opposite side of the basement door was a hallway with office doors on either side.

One of those doors was open. A light—surely the same light he had first seen from the parking lot—poured out, making a yellow triangle on the hall floor.

The light wasn't ominous. It wasn't foreboding. It didn't signal danger.

"Hello?" he asked once more as he rapped lightly on the open door.

But no one was inside.

The office, strangely, looked only recently vacated. But Gregory had worked at the bank for a good ten years at that point, and in all that time, he had never known of anyone working down here.

Still, Gregory could not find a speck of dust anywhere. No cobwebs. No dried-out and cracked leather. Why, the leather spines on the books behind the desk looked supple.

And if he wasn't cleaning the basement, who was?

The office also seemed old-fashioned—almost like it could have been set up as a display in the history museum. The bookcases that housed those large volumes were the sort that Gregory had only seen in antique stores—lawyer's bookcases, the kind with glass fronts. And on the desk sat a candlestick phone that was still plugged into the wall.

"What—?" Gregory started. Searching for a rational

explanation, he glanced at the door. The nameplate read, "Arthur K. Pulcheck, Esquire."

From the window, Gregory heard a few light taps. He realized the shade covering the small window near the ceiling had been pulled back, the flap tucked behind a scales of justice sculpture. Had someone just done that? Is that why no one had ever been able to see in from the outside, know there was still an office in the basement?

But who?

Gregory inched closer. Tugged the chain on a nearby light—a lovely thing with a brass base and a rather ornate glass shade. Something Tina would have placed right inside the entrance at the It Ain't Over Yet flea market.

There, on the tiny sill, sat a cardinal. Bright red.

The color of Christmas, Gregory caught himself thinking.

He was about to leave when the bird's tapping grew louder, more insistent. Gregory couldn't explain why, but he had an overwhelming sensation that this cardinal was trying to tell him something. Or maybe just get him to notice something.

"What do you want, little fella?" Gregory asked, looking up and down the office.

He paced a bit, and swore that the tapping grew still louder and faster when he was closest to the desk.

"Oh, of all the ridiculous—Gregory," he scolded himself, "you've lost it."

But there *was* an envelope placed in the exact center of the desk. Right there on the old-fashioned leather desk protector, the kind with the black corners. The yellowing envelope read, in a thick black ink, the letters a somewhat antique, flowery script, "To Whom it May Concern."

Gregory stared a moment, certain that the letter wasn't for him—or was it? "I suppose I'm as good a 'whom' as anyone," Gregory said out loud. "And I don't think I'm concerned, exactly, but I'm sure curious." He looked up at the cardinal, who had stopped tapping. "That's close enough, isn't it? I qualify, right?"

Gregory picked up the envelope, flipped it over, and tugged the letter free.

"Walter Drummond," Gregory said, reading the name at the top of the stationery. Scott's father.

The letter couldn't have been written long before Walter'd died. It rambled a bit, but there were several references to family. The need to preserve things. To write things down. To have a back-up plan. (*But for what?* Gregory wondered.) Walter recalled in the letter that his own journey—the best one he took in his life—had begun right there. In Pulcheck's office. And he had one more very important message to leave behind.

After this pronouncement, though, the page contained only a string of numbers.

"That's it?" Gregory asked, flipping the page over and finding it blank. "Numbers?"

It seemed like some sort of code, almost.

At any rate, whatever Walter wanted to say was lost on Gregory.

"Think I should show this to Scott?" he asked the cardinal. "This letter might make some sense to him. And he was just telling me how much he misses his dad." Gregory reexamined the letter. "Then again, maybe he won't be able to make heads or tails of this, either. Maybe it'll only make him even sadder to know he never got to find out what this was all about. What do you think?"

But the cardinal had no advice to give. He simply took off.

"You got to go to the Ruby's Place opening, too?" Gregory muttered.

He tested the strength of the old desk chair, leaning and pressing on it a few different times before deciding to give it his full weight. He climbed onto the seat to straighten the shade behind the scales of justice statue.

Gregory took the letter with him, wondering once more how that office could have been left so perfectly preserved. Why hadn't anyone wanted to move in? Why hadn't anyone at least cleaned it out?

He reached behind him to kill the light, but it flickered and died before he could find the switch. As soon as he stepped into the hallway, the door fell shut behind him. When Gregory reached for the doorknob, it refused to turn. Locked.

He climbed the same stairs that had taken him down to the basement. On the ground floor, Gregory searched for a wall clock. How much time had he wasted wandering around in the basement? He checked the ornate, antique wall clock (bronze, made especially for the Bank of Sullivan, with a gilded "Est. 1901" curling along the base). It told him he had only spent a couple of minutes down there.

Behind him, a second door—this time, the door to the basement—slammed. Locked.

Not that it mattered. "I have promises to keep," Gregory announced. He rattled the letter at the old portrait of Walter, still on the wall next to the clock. "I promised your son."

Below the wall clock—and Walter's portrait—the ancient vault stood silently, protecting every secret it still had inside.

Gregory folded the letter, placed it in the center of Scott's desk, and added a note: "Found this straightening the basement a bit," he wrote in part. "Looks to be from your dad."

He snatched his suit off the teller's booth and headed to the men's room.

What Gregory had not noticed was that when Walter's letter had grown close to the vault—in those brief seconds before he'd folded it up—the numbers Walter had scrawled had sparkled a bright silver, the color of brand-new tinsel.

16.

DECEMBER 16, 1938

WALTER'S MOTHER TOSSED the wooden box Mr. Pulcheck had given them into the barrel in the backyard, the same old ancient rusting metal bin where Walter's parents stacked their newspapers and yard waste to be burned. She snorted and grumbled about that crazy old Bonwit couple (it was *couple* now, not just *Mrs.*). First, Hetty chases Walter away by screaming and swinging that broom of hers, threatening bodily harm, and then Mr. Bonwit bequeaths him a whopping three dollars (not nothing, especially during rough times, but certainly not enough to change a family's life) and a ridiculous story.

"They were crazier than any of us ever could have suspected," his mother spat, brushing off her hands. "It's a good thing none of this came out while they were still alive." As though she would take some revenge, if only she could go back in time. She punctuated this sentence with a slam of the back screen door.

Her words brought a fresh round of shame to Walter. But he was relieved that the only people his mother spoke *to* regarding the whole inheritance fiasco were Walter and his father. The fact that she had actually gone out to the attorney's office—and gotten her hopes up when the word "inheritance" had hit the air—was embarrassing to her. Downright mortifying. It painted her as the world's most gullible person, salivating in her best hat with the cherries on the brim.

Such a silly woman, the people of Sullivan would have all said, shaking their heads—their remarks not about Mrs. Bonwit, but about Walter's mother.

She knew that would be the case. And so she left her disgust at the mudroom door, deposited it with the dirty shoes and the wet coats, never to be trotted out to be seen by the good people of Sullivan.

Walter stared at the burn bin through his bedroom window. It was a torture for him, knowing that the old music box was just sitting out there where anyone could take it. Now, with Mrs. Bonwit gone, maybe everyone would decide that every backyard in the town of Sullivan was up for grabs. Maybe they would all decide that fences never should have meant anything, anyway.

Maybe some boy—even Petey himself—would stride through the Drummond yard on his way to the park, spy the Bonwits' wooden box, and driven by curiosity, open to take a peek inside.

Walter's mother had been so perturbed at the whole thing, she hadn't even taken the three dollars out.

Walter couldn't quite explain why he wanted it. It wasn't the three dollars. Not really. Perhaps he wanted it simply because it had been left to him. At ten, few things in life were given to a boy by someone other than his best friend or his parents. That was Walter's wooden box, not his mother's. It didn't seem fair to him that his own box should be tossed in order for his mother to somehow save face.

After dark, he crept in his pajamas down to the base of the stairs. He slipped into his coat and out the door.

The night smelled like Christmas, like pine and chimney smoke. The snow crunched beneath his leather slippers and the cold air swirled about his ankles.

He leaned over the rim of the barrel and gasped. In the dark, it appeared that the box was not there.

That couldn't be true, though, or so he told himself. He plunged deeper into the barrel, swirling his hands about. His fingertips scraped against the jagged ends of sticks and swirled across the rough twists of twine holding stacks of newspapers together. All of it waiting for Mr. Drummond's match to turn it into ash.

But Walter didn't want his box—if it was even still there—to be incinerated. Surely, he thought, it had simply fallen down beneath the top layer. Surely it hadn't already been stolen. It just couldn't have.

He needed a light. He raced back toward the house, up the stairs to retrieve his camping lantern.

But he stopped in the doorway of his bedroom.

A light was already shining. Pouring onto the Bonwits' wooden box, which was now sitting on Walter's bed in a nest of crumpled blankets.

Walter stopped, his arms held out slightly from his sides, his eyes wide, his heart galloping at a strange, frantic pace.

How could the box have beaten me upstairs? he wondered.

And then the light simply disappeared.

Walter sat across from his father at the next morning's break-fast table, wanting to ask if he was the one who had rescued the box. But he didn't dare in front of his mother. He tried to watch his father over the rim of his orange juice glass for some hint, some sign that it had been him. He wanted his father to hold his gaze the instant his mother turned her back to stir the oatmeal on the stove. He wanted his father to share a smirk or a wink.

But there was nothing.

It had to have been him, though. Didn't it? Somehow? His father could have been watching and beaten Walter up the stairs. Couldn't he? When Walter had paused in the mud-room to knock the snow from his slippers so that his moth-er wouldn't notice puddles? Couldn't that have been when it happened? And the beam of light, why, that was simply a strip of moonlight filtering in through his window. And the reason it had suddenly disappeared? Well, it had been obscured by a cloud.

Simple explanations all around.

…Then why couldn't Walter wholly believe *any* of it?

Now, with the box securely in his possession, he found he had zero interest in the money. It was Bonwit's instruc-tions that had his attention. Maybe poor Mr. Bonwit had been driven completely mad by his change in fortune. Maybe he loved his Hetty enough to convince himself that this box would save her, when he himself could not.

But it was such a fun idea—that giving money away would allow you to keep it. What was the harm in trying it out? It was Saturday, freeing up an entire day for Walter's experiment.

After breakfast, Walter pulled one of the dollar bills from the box. He held it in his open palm, waiting for a sign of some sort. If it had the ability to regenerate itself, shouldn't it have trembled or turned warm against his skin?

He carried it to the window, to see if the December sun would do something to it. He brought it to his closet and held it in the dark. But the strange glow he'd sworn he'd seen the night before—the same he'd dismissed as moonlight, but now wondered about—didn't show itself again.

Walter couldn't help but think he was being fooled yet again. That if he kept going, he would wind up feeling every bit as embarrassed and angry as his mother had been in Mr. Pulcheck's office.

He squinted at the dollar bill, which looked incredibly ordinary. And well-worn. A bit crinkly. Soft around the edges. Folded into half and then quarters multiple times. Which meant it had been used to buy who-knew-what already. Perhaps it had been handed over in order to help pay rent, or to buy children's shoes. Groceries. Perhaps a family's lunch at Frankie's diner. And no one had ever hinted at having found something magical in their cash register drawers.

If the magic was in the money, shouldn't someone else have seen this magic before?

Walter glanced behind his shoulder. Maybe, he thought, the magic was in the box. He picked it up, turning it about in his hands. But it was nothing, really. As Pulcheck had indicated, it did in fact appear to be a broken music box, one that had had its guts removed at one point. The metal piece on the bottom that had once wound the box was still there, somehow frozen in place.

No music would ever play from it again.

But something was still pressing Walter forward. He put a dollar bill in his pocket—pausing one more time for some sort of sign that something magical was about to unfold—then picked up a few extra coins from his own savings. After all, to truly test this, he couldn't spend even one cent on himself. He had to spend that dollar on somebody else. He shrugged himself inside his coat, and headed out into the frosty morning air.

Petey was coming down his front steps as Walter made his way through the neighborhood.

"Smells like snow," Walter said in greeting.

Petey scoffed. "You sound like my grandfather with that corny stuff."

Walter made a face, and the two of them laughed as they hurried down the street, off to their movie day. A day of flickering lights and cheap B-movies, those Poverty Row quickies that spanned less than an hour before the theater coughed them back up into the street. Their one-Saturday-a-month treat.

Walter made sure to be ahead of Petey when they reached the front of the ticket counter. He slid his own shiny coin forward, retrieved his ticket, then told Petey, "You know what? My treat," and slid the magical dollar bill toward the girl in the booth.

"Thanks, Walt," Petey said, taking the ticket.

Inside, the lobby smelled of popcorn and snowy shoulders.

Walter rushed to the concession stand and returned with a Krackle bar, a butter-leaking bag of popcorn, and a paper cup of Coca-Cola.

"What's this for?" Petey asked as Walter pushed it all

into his hands.

"Krackle's your favorite," Walter said with a shrug. "And it's Christmas, and we're pals."

Petey eyed him with skepticism, which soon bled into a pool of something close to worry. "You sure you're okay?" he asked. "You seem almost sick or something."

Walter did feel a little sick. Dizzy. But it was only because of the speed with which his hopes were spinning through him. He sweated and he swayed on his feet. But he flashed a crooked smile and nudged Petey into the theater.

He still had plenty of dollar left, though. So after the movie, he bought Petey an *Action Comic* with Superman on the cover and a balsa wood plane complete with elastic band to make it fly.

"Boy, oh, boy," Petey said as they walked home. "I didn't know you were going to do all this. What a Christmas! On your birthday…" he started to promise, since Walter's birthday was well into spring, giving him time to work up a big surprise. But Walter knew that Petey's pockets were perpetually empty. He was a sucker for drugstore goodies and terrible at marbles. Most of any money he happened to get his hands on went to buying cheap commies in order to be let into games out on the blacktop.

Walter didn't care about Petey evening the score. Now that he had spent the entirety of the dollar, he only cared about the story he'd heard in Mr. Pulcheck's office. As they walked, closing in on their neighborhood, he reached into his pocket, his fingers trembling as he searched the folds. He wanted to feel it again—the soft edges of a dollar bill.

But there was nothing. He had spent the whole thing on Petey, and in return, all he had was an empty pocket.

The money had not magically replenished itself.

Walter's heart pumped a stinging anger. But he couldn't exactly direct it at Hetty. She might not have even known about the box, not if she'd never needed it during her lifetime. And he was too busy feeling sorry for Mr. Bonwit to be mad at him. So Walter turned his anger toward Mr. Pulcheck, that ridiculous dusty relic of a lawyer locked in the basement of the Bank of Sullivan. He fantasized about bursting into the office, and there Mr. Pulcheck would be, looking dustier than ever. Like some forgotten piece of paper in a file that had slid down inside his metal cabinet. Half-melted beeswax candles would slump on his bookshelf behind him. The candlestick phone would sit silent. Who would ever need to call him, especially now that Mrs. Bonwit was gone?

"You didn't have to go along with it," Walter would admonish, pointing a righteous finger at him. "Mrs. Bonwit was mean, and Mr. Bonwit was not—not—*not of sound mind.*" (Hadn't he heard that somewhere—maybe not at Pulcheck's, but in one of his Saturday movies?) "You didn't have to honor ridiculous last wishes," he would tell Pulcheck. "Stringing me along like that. To think you would punish the only person in the entire town who showed up to Mrs. Bonwit's funeral!"

Mr. Pulcheck would curl into himself, shame evident. And Walter would simply turn on his heel and slam the door, leaving the man to rot in an office as dark and dank as a mole's home.

Petey was riding high on sugar and his unexpected good fortune. "Let's not go home yet. Come on. We've got time," he pleaded.

But Walter was worn out. He wanted to forget this awful, embarrassing thing—believing in the Bonwits. He understood exactly how his mother had felt after the meeting with Pulcheck. Now Walter wanted to hide his hope like it had never happened, too.

Walter and Petey parted ways. The cold burned Walter's lungs, but in a good way. The air was a reminder that he was such a young boy with so much time left, which was far more than could be said for the rotten Bonwits. They had run out of time, out of air. They were food for worms, and what had they done other than leave behind lies and meanness? Walter never would. He would never be that kind of person, and he had so much time in which to prove it.

Walter raced through his front door. As he climbed the stairs, he hummed "Memories of You," his father's favorite.

Memories of everyone but Mrs. Bonwit was more like it, Walter thought sourly. He needed to scratch her existence from his mind completely. Time to put this whole silly business behind him.

In his bedroom doorway, Walter's voice caught in his throat, killing his song. The box was on his bed. Open.

Had he really left it that way? Hadn't he shoved it—well—*somewhere?* Into his closet? Under the bed? Granted, he'd been in a hurry to get out of the house and try the money story out, but surely he would have put the box somewhere that a dusting or bed-straightening or clothes-putting-away mother would never go.

Wouldn't he?

Walter edged his way inside his room. The floor creaked beneath him, seeming to offer high-pitched warnings.

"I gave the whole dollar away," Walter whispered to the open box. When it didn't answer, Walter pressed, "Did you hear me?"

Somehow, it seemed to. Somehow, Walter thought that the box was about to speak.

Laugh at him, was more like it.

A new anger flushed hot inside him—an anger at himself. Why did he keep behaving like such a little boy? Walter lunged forward, grabbed the box, and shoved it under his bed. He plopped down on the edge, the mattress sagging beneath him, and he placed his head in his hands. Why did his heart always do this to him? Why did he always find himself believing, over and over, when he shouldn't? Why could his heart never learn?

Only—what was that thing he'd seen, in the moment he'd flipped the lid shut? Something shiny?

He bent down, head between legs, to pull that box back out from under the bed.

Walter undid the brass latch. And there, inside, were three dollars. Not two, as there should have been after Walter had removed one. Three.

And one extra, very shiny, very new Mercury dime.

17.

DECEMBER 24, 2018

"I WASN'T THE UNLUCKY SOD I'd once thought," Walter said.

Scott only stared at him in shock, trying to absorb this strange story his father had just related of having inherited a magical box.

"No one else knew," Walter went on. "From the outside, the years trudged on, and it appeared as though nothing had changed, not for me. From the outside, I'm sure it looked as though my bad luck just kept following me. Each new school term brought some disaster or another. Disappointing bad marks, occasionally even in my best subjects. Boyish fistfights and purple lips. Broken hearts from young girls when I got a little older. Summers still scorched my skin and winters still stung me through my boots."

Walter sipped his scotch. "But there was always the box, which I took great pains to hide from a mother occasionally overzealous about her cleaning. Often, it was taped to the back of my desk. Or behind my copy of *Treasure Island*. I took to collecting music boxes at one point—which Mother thought was quite charming, I recall. I became over-the-top about it, polishing the wood and taking great care with the inner machinery. That way, I could leave the Bonwit box out in the open, and know that Mother would respect it enough to leave it alone. She thought that old box Pulcheck had given us was long gone. I can't tell you how proud I was of that music box collection idea."

Walter paused to smile at the ideas of his younger self. "At any rate," he went on, "that box convinced me that no matter what disaster struck, I wasn't unlucky at all."

"You—you kept using it?" Scott stammered. The first thing he'd said since Walter had begun his story.

"The first Christmas gave me plenty of cover," Walter explained. "I was supposed to be buying gifts, anyway. It was the right time of the year for it. And each time I gave something, I got a little back. By the time the new year rolled around, I began to think maybe I could indulge myself…or could I?"

"Not if you didn't want to tamper with it. Break the spell," Scott said.

Walter smiled with relief. "That's right," he whispered.

"What did you do?" Scott pressed. "Did you keep going?"

"I started doing things in secret," Walter said. "I became—well—depending on your point of view, I was either a real sleuth or an eavesdropper. Listening for gossip—and in Sullivan, there's always gossip. I overheard discussions while waiting in line to buy stamps at the post office. I listened in when whispers were exchanged in the library. I hung around the front of the old hardware store. I heard it all. Who was having trouble. Whose husband lost his job. Who got robbed, even. I took to leaving money in mailboxes or coat pockets. The bigger the gift, I found, the bigger the return."

"You must have had *so much money*," Scott said, clearly in awe. "I mean, you were just a kid at first, but if you were giving gifts big enough to rescue adults with their money problems when you were still a boy…"

"Oh, it couldn't all fit inside my box anymore," Walter said, sliding a small wooden object out of a shadow. "I had to start putting the money somewhere else. Someplace truly safe."

"Like the bank," Scott whispered, his face shifting as a new realization hit. "You started the community fund with it. Didn't you? When you were grown?"

"I used it to loan Ruby the money she needed to open this very place," Walter agreed. "And then I loaned the money I got back to her friend Elizabeth to open a dress shop. And so on."

"But did Ruby—or anyone else you loaned to from the community fund—know that it was getting replenished even before they paid their loans back?"

"Of course not."

"So it got paid double?"

"I couldn't let on about the fund. I couldn't let anyone know. What if, by telling the story, I killed the magic? I had to let them pay it back like it was a regular loan," Walter said.

"What about the people who hit hard times with their business? Didn't you ever have one that fell apart? Someone that went belly-up?"

"You know," Walter said, leaning closer to his son, "it was just the strangest thing. Every single time someone started to have trouble, money would show up, inexplicably, in their hour of need." And he winked.

Scott laughed. "The ultimate fool-proof investment."

Walter shrugged sheepishly.

They stared at each other a moment. It had been so long since Walter had seen his son. It was really something to be talking to him now like two men. In Walter's current state, in his all-time favorite suit with the wide lapels, his hair full of those streaks of gray that made him look distinguished instead of worn-out, he reflected an age that was barely older than that of his own boy.

Walter took in every inch of his son—the wedding band, the close shave, the laugh lines. He noted with pride that Scott was even wearing Walter's old tie tack. Walter had *raised* this person. He had taught him how to tie his shoes and turn the other cheek and open doors for anyone weighed down by an armload of packages or a bulging briefcase or a wiggling child.

And now, here Scott was, a man who paid taxes and knew how to drive and mow the lawn and cook dinner and corral children at the pediatrician.

It was a marvel, really, how that had happened.

As proud as Walter was, part of him also missed the little boy who had accompanied him on Christmas Eve, who had taken such pride in his first boutonnière and three-piece suit. Who had looked to Walter as though adulthood was a secret that needed unlocking.

And yet, Walter told himself, his thoughts circling around again, here they were. The keys to all those secrets were now with Scott. They were his to pass down to his own children. It was, Walter thought, both the natural expected way of things and also a miracle.

"And it all started when you were ten," Scott muttered,

revealing that his own thoughts were traveling down similar paths. "It's sort of hard to think of you as a little boy," he admitted. "To think of you as a ten-year-old. I *have* a kid who's nearly ten years old."

"Sometimes," Walter admitted, "when I was grown, I did miss being a boy. Especially when you were young and tromping about. It wasn't about baseball and bicycles, though. I just missed having a part of life that was mine alone. That was how childhood worked back when I was young—the front door flew open and you were trusted to join the rest of the children as they all raced out toward their own mysterious lives, the ones that belonged only to them, that no parents had access to.

"It was a delicious sort of privacy, really. I only realized it years later, of course, when I was getting up in the morning and smearing my face with shaving cream, listening to the usual family sounds. Oh, *you know,*" Walter said, acknowledging Scott's place in life, "the breakfast bowls rattling in the cabinet and that infernal television, which gabs all day long, doesn't it?"

Scott offered the tiniest of nods.

"You listen to your own kids and you marvel at the way none of childhood had seemed even remotely special from the viewpoint of a child. It seems ordinary when you're in the midst of it. It's the travesty of life to realize such things only after chapters of life have wrapped."

"It—it is," Scott agreed.

"Time is a terrible thing," Walter told Scott. Now that he was talking, he had so much he wanted him to know. "Like a sweetheart that eventually changes her mind about you and turns her back. Yes, time is a fickle sweetheart," he bellowed, sweeping his arms in a grand gesture. "It leaves you and then…"

"Then you're just…gone," Scott finished.

After a pause, Scott continued, "Only, you're not. Are you? You're not gone. You're here now. Like something out of Dickens, really. You're here. And this is the story you choose to tell me. A story about a woman you barely ever spoke about before. Bonwit—I know you said you got the community fund from her, but nothing else. Nothing about this box. Not ever, when we were both…" He wrinkled his brow. "Why? Why now, I mean? When you started, you acted like you had the most important thing to tell me."

"Because you're going to tear down the bank."

"How did you know about that?" Scott asked.

"You'll destroy the vault, son, don't you see? You can't destroy the vault."

"But nobody's been in it for years. It can't have anything important in it."

"Important!" Walter's eyes flamed with anger and fear. "What did I used to tell you was in the vault?" Walter asked.

"You—you said—" Scott was a bit rattled by this question. Staring into Walter's eyes, though, the answer came to him. "You said—the vault didn't just have money. You said it held deeds and investments and hopes. A whole town's dreams. It was somebody's house where they'd raise their kids. It was a new business that would go into an empty space in one of those old buildings on the square. It was an education. You said it was tomorrow. That's what was in the vault—tomorrow."

"I did. But I was only partially right. It also held inheritances and antique coins and gold wedding rings from three generations ago. It held the past, too."

"It held memories," Scott said.

"So many memories," Walter agreed. "But it's been so long now that some of *us* are memories. Us. People like me. You see?"

Scott wasn't quite sure.

"A person is alive as long as their memory is alive. Sometimes, memories have to be put away for safekeeping. People lose everything if it's not under lock and key. They're terrible, even with the most precious things. Birth certificates. Marriage licenses. Family heirlooms."

"And memories," Scott finished.

"And memories," Walter said.

"The vault holds memories," Scott said. And he snorted through his nose. "This is one of your old puns, isn't it?" he asked. "The memory bank. Come on, Dad."

Walter blanched. Surely Scott wasn't starting to discount what he'd told him, was he? He had to act fast, before Scott's belief started to wane.

"What's keeping the people of Sullivan from turning out?" Walter asked. "Why isn't anyone else here yet? Why is that street out there empty?"

Scott shook his head, not sure what Walter was getting at.

"Why are *you* here?" Walter asked.

"Because—I…" Scott's mind spun. He thought of the tarnished tinsel and the emptiness of the aluminum snowflakes and the hollowness that had invaded him a holiday season long. But in here, in the place where his memories felt the closest, he had a different feeling. It was one of warmth and excitement. The past was not far here. It was as though he had circled back around, to something sweet and lovely. Had those bad feelings of his been nothing other than frustration? Anger at the fact that, like Walter had just said, a chapter of his life had closed before he'd had the ability to understand just how precious it was?

Walter raised an eyebrow, waiting for an answer. "Well?" he pressed. "Why are you here?"

"I remember," Scott whispered.

"You remember," Walter said. "In vivid detail. You remember how wonderful it was on Christmas here. And the reason is because you've been going over it in your mind. Replaying it. But over time, if you don't replay memories, they fade. They grow as hazy as a winter-fogged window. They've forgotten, Scottie. Everybody in town. They've forgotten so much of what went on inside Ruby's."

"But what can I do—?" Scott started.

"I made a withdrawal earlier tonight," Walter said, tapping the top of his old broken-down music box, the same with the winder that had been frozen for a century.

"That thing—it has—"

"All the memories of Christmas Eve at Ruby's Place," Walter said. "And we need to remind Sullivan. So they'll come to the Ruby's Place reopening."

"They've forgotten," Scott murmured, trying to keep all the pieces of the story together in his mind.

"Let's remind them," he told Scott, pushing the box closer to him.

18.

"GO ON," WALTER SAID, nudging Scott. "Open it."

Slowly, Scott lifted the lid.

The metal piece on the bottom—frozen in place since Walter had inherited it—began to twirl.

And music started to play.

But not a kind of music that could be heard. This was only music that could be felt, from the deepest part inside Scott. As though heartstrings were an actual instrument. A harp or a lute, maybe, and they were suddenly being strummed.

He laughed at the sensation. *Heartstrings.* A pun his father would love.

And then, something else happened to him.

He felt it. The Christmas spirit, that feeling that he'd thought was gone forever. That overwhelming sensation of security and belonging and…well, love. Wasn't that mostly it? Just—love. Not only receiving love, either. But loving other people. In that way he had as a child, all open arms and no fear.

Wasn't that the gift, really? The one they always talked about on Christmas—*better to give than receive?* Wasn't it always about love? Didn't it feel better to love someone than to receive it?

What was love without giving it first?

"I—I have so much to tell you," Scott said, tears gathering. "I—my kids—my wife. I have to get them."

"No," Walter said. "You don't understand. Scott. I can't. I can't do this forever. We all had an understanding. The regulars and I. I could only have one meeting with you, and this is what I had to show you. The bank, you see. After tonight, I'll return the memories. The vault—"

"No," Scott said. "Please. Don't go anywhere. I'll be right back."

19.

THE SOUND OF FOOTSTEPS brought Angela out from the kitchen. "Hello?" she called. "Is someone here?"

On the bar, though, was only the scotch she had initially poured and an empty wooden box.

"Walter?" Angela tried, glancing about.

She frowned at the scotch neat still sitting on the bar's edge—and a handkerchief of ice wadded next to the glass. "Walter?" she repeated, more tentative that time.

Standing there, beside the odd, open box, it all flooded her again—the same sensations she'd had on Christmas Eves with her Aunt Elizabeth. Dressed in whatever lovely ensemble her aunt had plucked from the shelves of her own dress store, the one she'd owned since being granted that life-changing loan from Walter Drummond at the bank. She remembered the silk stockings and the gowns and the trinkets—maybe a pin or scarf for her coat, a smell-good to dab on her wrists.

She remembered Scott Drummond being at Ruby's with his father. How she and Scott had exchanged surprised glances at one another, neither one of them looking quite like themselves outside of their tennis shoes and their blue jeans.

She remembered the feeling of believing. Not in Santa or fairy tales, but in herself. Believing that she was a special one. That life was about to open and welcome her. All she had to do was reach out.

She laughed at the memory. And she marveled at the fact that suddenly, somewhere deep inside, those old feelings were with her again.

She walked to the entrance and threw it open, glancing up and down the street as the burst of yesterdays swirled, dancing down the pavement and skipping across the face of every decades-old decoration. Rewinding the damage time had done. Making everything look new and sparkly again.

20.

A BURST OF YESTERDAYS SWIRLED, splitting and shooting in hundreds of glittering directions, all through the unsuspecting town of Sullivan. It slinked across streets and down chimneys and through the tiny grooves in front door keyholes.

Suddenly, in kitchens, couples put down the dishes they had been planning to place on their tables. They exchanged glances. *Do we really want to eat at home tonight?* they asked each other.

Before they could answer, one of their phones pinged. They'd find a friend or coworker had just texted. *Didn't you plan on going to Ruby's?*

They hadn't. But why? What was the reason? What could have kept them from the grand reopening? Hadn't they once loved their own Christmas Eves at Ruby's? Hadn't they all been gossiping about it for a year solid?

Laughing and squealing like the children they had once been, they raced each other for their bedrooms to attack closets, pulling out their very best dresses and even the stockings no one bothered with anymore. Standing before the mirror, they held a parade of ties next to their chosen shirts. Cuff links were dug from the bottoms of jewelry boxes.

They screwed on the backs of their grandmother's pearl earrings. They dabbed wrists with the cologne they'd set aside for special occasions. They made bargains with the kids: *I know I told you Santa wanted you in bed, but I was wrong. He wants you to come with us. To a special place. With special treats just for you.*

As they reached for their coats, the sent their own texts, this time to residents were far too young to have ever spent a Christmas Eve in Ruby's Place.

No excuses, they implored, *you have to come. It's going to be a night to remember.*

The urgency was too powerful to ignore. Wave after wave of residents piled into their cars, and somehow, to each one of them, it seemed that the streets had been cleared just for them. It didn't matter that the snow plows had been out all day, snaking through Sullivan, making multiple rounds. No reasonable answer to anything would be accepted, not tonight.

It was back, somehow. The warm, happy feeling that Christmas had, in years long gone, brought to them all. The simple belief that wishes would be answered. Why not? It was Christmas Eve.

Yes, Christmas was here. The Christmas of old. The Christmas so many had assumed was gone for good.

Everyone—every single person, throughout Sullivan, regardless of age—could smell and taste its sweetness.

21.

GREGORY WAS HALFWAY ACROSS the parking lot when something—out of the ordinary? Unusual? Oh, call it what it was. Something truly *miraculous* happened.

That was how he would always think of it, long after presents had been opened and decorations had been put away yet again, shoved back into darkened corners of storage. The night the great pragmatist, who had always before been able to find a plausible explanation that could instantly remove every hint of magic from the world, could find no rational answer.

As he was standing in the lot, the silver tinsel wrapped around the parking lot light poles grew brighter. And brighter. Strands trembled in the winter breeze, catching the moonlight and throwing sprays of metallic light across Gregory's shoulders.

Across the street, the owner of The Page Turner bookstore waved and called to him, "Merry Christmas!" The soft tinkle of bells attached to the front door of the It Ain't Over Yet flea market sounded suddenly not like random high-pitched tones, but an actual melody. A new carol that cried out to be transcribed to sheet music.

It came back to Gregory—those last-minute shopping sprees he'd once gone on with his father, their mad scramble to get all the present-buying finished on Christmas Eve. He remembered how the square had bustled on those nights, not with panic and the burden of having to spend money, but with utter joy. The shoppers, he recalled, hadn't battled each other on Christmas Eve. They'd laughed and raced across stores to hug one another. On more than one occasion, a fellow Sullivanite had carried a gift across a store floor, calling out Gregory's father's name. Their own next-door neighbor had once appeared with a scarf in her hand, promising, "This will look fantastic with the Mrs.'s new coat." Another year, the town librarian appeared with a pair of earrings that he said would match the reading glasses Gregory's mother always wore as a necklace.

Gregory had joined in, dragging fathers to toy aisles and pointing, telling them what their own sons—his best friends—had *really* whispered into Santa's ear, when they'd sat on his lap in the middle of Sears.

Gregory remembered, too, how the old dime store had been a shopping paradise for himself and his sister, where a dollar saved could buy a gift that would make their own father gasp or laugh and draw them both in for one of his famous hugs on Christmas morning.

He remembered the can't-wait feeling of buying a gift, how he'd looked forward to seeing the expression on the face of each gift's recipient. Even neighborhood streets were full as they'd driven home from their Christmas Eve shopping excursions. All those Merry Christmas honks of the horns, the shouts out of car windows. *Everything* had overflowed back then.

Well, everything but the town Christmas tree lot, which had scarcely a pine needle left.

And then, there was dinner at Ruby's Place. Always Ruby's Place, the perfect ending to the perfect Christmas Eve.

Old scenes continued to play out in Gregory's mind, in bright Technicolor. On the other side of the parking lot, light moved up and down the tinsel, making the silver strands shimmer as if in anticipation of everything this night had in store.

Gregory no longer regretted telling Scott he would see him at Ruby's. Now, like the boy he'd once been, he couldn't wait to get there. And, like the boy he'd once been, he turned in the direction of Ruby's Place, and he started to run.

22.

FROM THE LIVING ROOM of the old Bonwit place, Brian called out, "Sir? Sir?"

"You're all right, aren't you?" Peter's high-pitched voice answered from the porch. "You're not hurt in there, are you?"

Brian laughed, his voice echoing through the empty home. "You act as though this is a house of horrors. Full of torture chambers and booby traps."

"I half-expect it to be."

"You really haven't set foot inside this house?" Brian asked.

"Nope."

"Mr. Collins, it's lovely. From what I can see, anyway. What I wouldn't give to have—say—a flashlight…"

"Oh, no, you don't," Peter shouted. "I see what you're doing. You want my flashlight, you come get it."

"Really, Mr. Collins," Brian said. "I'd love for you to see this old place."

Something odd had happened to Brian upon stepping inside the old Bonwit home. An overwhelming sense of pure want had enveloped him—as well as a sense of urgency. Of needing to act quickly. To make this Victorian jewel his own.

But do what with it? Brian wasn't sure, exactly. It wasn't as though he wanted to move to Sullivan—did he? Or start a business here—right?

"Pete!" Brian shouted. He wasn't sure if the man ever went by a shortened version of his name. But so much of Brian's work involved public relations. Becoming a friend of the town in which his company wanted to make a giant footprint. "Seriously. I know there's a part of you that's dying to know what's inside. After all this time?"

Silence.

"Pete. Come on. It's a house, man. It's not a superstition, you know? It's not—a ladder that shouldn't be walked under, or a mirror that should never be touched because you might break it. There's no bad luck here. Just the opposite. You gotta see this."

The floor began to creak in the area of the front door. Footsteps, Brian knew.

And then, instead of a man walking inside, the flashlight skittered across the floor. Peter had placed it on the ground and pushed it.

Brian picked up the light and swung it about, taking in the interior. After a few minutes, he carried it outside. "It's beautiful," he said softly. "You'd fall in love with it if you saw it."

"I dunno," Peter admitted. At this point, he was no longer even standing on the porch, but a few feet down the front walk. "To me, it's still a little…creepy, honestly. You have to understand, I never replaced my feelings about Mrs. Bonwit with anything else. Those feelings are still here, probably because *I'm* here. Maybe if I had moved somewhere else, and didn't have to look at this house every single day, I would have forgotten it. I would have forgotten the way she shooed us all away, and how angry we were at the way she treated us, but how it made us afraid, too. I don't know, maybe just the bad stuff would have faded and I would have remembered something else. Something like riding bikes down this street with my friend."

Peter gestured toward the street. He started to turn back toward Brian, but stopped. He just stood there, in his pajamas, in the freezing night air, staring at the same street he had traveled every day of his life.

"That's funny," Peter said.

"What is?"

"What I just said. I would have remembered riding bikes with my friend," he repeated, in a tone laced with awe.

"Excuse me?"

"It just—*it hit me,*" Peter confessed. "I don't know why. Just now. Maybe because of the fact that I'm here, talking about this place with so many ties to my boyhood, but…it's coming back to me."

"What is?" Brian asked.

"My best friend," Peter said. "From my childhood, I mean. The one I used to ride bikes with and walk to school with and play marbles with, all on this very street."

He pointed toward the Bonwit house, where the streetlight cast the silhouettes of two figures against the white exterior.

At first, Brian assumed it was the two of them—himself and Peter. But once he gave it a better look-over, it wasn't. Not even close. The two shadow figures were the shapes of boys. And they were leaning on the wrought iron fence along the edge of the yard.

Peter's face softened. "His name was Walter," he said.

"I haven't thought of him in ages. So odd how that happens. How someone so important to you at one point can fade. Even if your life is different, even if you've parted ways, that doesn't change what you were to each other once. It's so clear to me now, at this point in my life—but what is more important than friendship? It's more important than anything. More important than family, because it's chosen. Maybe even more important than romance, because romantic love can be fickle and selfish.

"Friendship," he repeated, taking a few steps closer to the flickering silhouettes.

"Walter," he whispered. "My old friend. We were both warned to stay away from this house—and we did—well, we sort of stayed away. We used to take this shortcut to the library right through there." Peter pointed, and Brian followed with the flashlight, aiming it at the easement.

"My God," Peter whispered. "I can hear his voice. I can smell the chimney smoke of those winter afternoons. I can taste the old cigarette in my mouth. I used to sneak them back then. And peppermint candies to cover the smell. I can remember. He was my friend. In a way you never have again."

"The friendships of our childhood are truly something special," Brian agreed.

"Walter was so kindhearted," Peter said. "He didn't tease me because I lived in a funeral parlor. Other boys didn't like it there. Used to back away from the house, refused to come in. Didn't like the idea of dead bodies in the basement. But Walter came. He probably didn't like it much, either. But he never let on. And he never made fun of me for it. He was that kind of person. You could count on Walter. I never had that again. I didn't know how special that was." After a few beats of silence, he scratched at the top of his head and asked,

"Why didn't I know?"

"Did Walter move away as a boy?" Brian guessed.

"No. He stayed right here. Just like me. Walter Drummond. Managed the bank. His son works there now."

"Scott," Brian said, surprised.

"How did you know?"

"I just had a meeting with him. His last meeting before the holiday. I had no idea his father worked there, too."

"He's long gone, my old friend Walter. Passed many years ago."

"Oh," Brian said. "I'm sorry."

"No, it's just—the last time I saw Walter was at Ruby's Place. It was Christmas Eve, and we were grown. Walter'd married and had Scott by then—I had a family, too. But Walter'd gone to college, and I didn't. Didn't even finish high school."

"Take up the family business?"

"Oh, no," Peter said. "No, I didn't want anything to do with that. I was a mechanic. I did all right for myself—you really didn't need a college degree to succeed back then. But Walter worked at a desk, and I never had a job where I didn't have to wash the grease off my hands at the end of the day."

"Work is work," Brian said, shrugging.

"That's what college men always say," Peter told him. "The rest of us know—you feel like you failed at something. I was embarrassed."

"If Walter was the way you described, though—coming to visit you in a funeral parlor, not allowing other boys to make fun of you—that surely wouldn't have bothered him."

"It didn't," Peter said. "It bothered me. So much, I let the embarrassment come between us."

He tilted his head at the silhouette—which Brian had

begun to recognize as Peter's memories somehow coming to life, right there, in front of them. "Why did I do that?" He seemed to be asking one of the boy's shadows, flickering there on the wall.

"I never went back to Ruby's Place again," Peter admitted.

Brian watched Peter take a few steps closer to the trembling silhouettes.

When Brian tried to follow Peter with the flashlight, illuminating the steps ahead for him, the boys disappeared.

Peter swiveled; in the moonlight, Brian could see the wide-eyed expression of hope smoothing out the man's face.

"Would you mind if we locked back up?" he asked Brian.

"Come again?"

"I can't explain it. I have such a strong urge to go again. It's opening night, you know. Ruby's Place. If I go change my clothes and get my wife, would you come with us?"

"Why me?"

"Because to the people of Sullivan, Ruby's Place was always special—and it just might be again. I'd forgotten that, for a while. But if you're going to work on this town…you should experience it for yourself. See what makes it tick. Especially on Christmas Eve."

23.

HEADLIGHTS TICKLED the edges of tinsel all through the town—tinsel that had been draped in scallops across the elementary school and the bank, tinsel that had been twisted around the bases of street signs and light poles.

That same tinsel sparkled again, for everyone. Just as it had years ago.

The past was back. It was alive.

Walter smiled from the shadows just beyond the front window of Ruby's Place.

It was working.

24.

"SCOTT," JENNIFER BARKED. "Scott. Can you hear me?"

He blinked into the cold, finding her face an inch from his own, her eyes wide and worried. Stars glittered just behind her head. Had they always been so bright?

Snow bit at his bare fingertips. Were his legs stretched out on the ground? Were Jennifer's legs under his back?

She wrapped her arms around him even tighter, attempting to draw him into a sitting position. "I've been trying to get you to open your eyes for what feels like forever," she said. She used her teeth to tug one of her gloves free and touched his forehead.

Scott winced.

"One of those big icicles hanging from the roof must have hit you in the head," she said. "When I got here, you were out completely. Maybe we should forget this tonight. Maybe you should let me take you to the ER."

It slowly began to sink in that Scott was in the alley. Outside Ruby's Place.

"No, no," he protested. "I just need a minute."

But his head throbbed as he sat up, telling him that

Jennifer might very well be right about the emergency room. He felt more like he'd been whacked with a baseball than a chunk of ice. He fought against the pounding ache, struggling to make sense of the evening. He hadn't been in this alley the whole time, had he? Hadn't he just been inside the bar? Talked to his dad? How could he have gone from sitting at the bar to lying in the alley without actually passing through the door?

Come to think of it, wasn't the better question *how could he have been talking to a long-deceased Walter at all?*

He grunted as he struggled to get to his feet, push himself off the ground.

"Scott!" Jennifer scolded.

But what was he doing wrong? Was he not supposed to get up at all? Just stay stretched out there on the pavement in the alley until New Year's?

She held her hands in a way that reminded him of how she'd held her hands near their children as they'd learned to walk, giving them the ability to take their own steps but being close enough for rescue should they need it.

Was he that unsteady?

His head swirled like it had when he was a boy and had just gotten off one of those twisting rides at the county fair.

"If not the hospital, then we should go home. I'll drive—" she started, but Scott waved her offer away.

"I promised Angela I'd come tonight," he said.

"You're not planning to stay, are you?" she asked, her tone implying just how boneheaded she regarded this particular plan.

"Of course. It's especially important now that it looks like no one else is coming, and—" He tilted his head to the side. "Are you laughing?"

She was. She was laughing so hard that she was leaning backward and pointing toward the way he had come.

"What?" he asked.

"You haven't seen. You got out of the car a few minutes too early."

She led him out of the alley.

The entire street in front of Ruby's Place was brimming with cars—cramming both lanes so that traffic was moving at a crawl. The sidewalks held children skipping and adults grabbing each other up into welcome hugs. The air clanked with the music of joyful honks and the refrains of "Meeeerry Chriiiistmaas!" bellowing out from rolled-down car windows. Snowflakes made more than a few tilt their heads back and stick out their tongues. One white-headed couple even twirled. Why did falling flakes always make kids want to dance—even kids on the farthest end of the "one to ninety-two" spectrum sung about in the old carol?

All Scott knew for sure was that his *bah-humbug* feelings were being chipped away by the giggles and the sounds of voices calling, "Hurry!"

A line stretched from the front door of Ruby's Place all the way down the street.

"Come on, you two! You promised we'd have fun. All we've done is sit forever in the car!" a young voice scolded.

When Scott looked in its direction, he found that Alessandra had apparently decided to put herself in charge. She'd wrangled the twins, who were standing now on either side of her. She clasped their hands, as though to keep them from running off.

"You're sure you're up to it," Jennifer asked, the worried look still on her face. "That was quite a hit."

"Wouldn't miss it for the world," Scott said.

Ahead, the glow of the restored red neon Ruby's Place sign washed across the snow. Scott smiled, so glad that Angela had brought the old sign back. It shone as brightly as the North Star, and it pointed the crowd in the direction of the freshly-painted green door.

Those on the sidewalk pushed Scott toward the front of the line. "You loaned her the money," they reasoned. "First dibs."

It didn't seem quite fair, really—or maybe he just didn't like all the attention—but Scott wasn't one to argue. Inside, Jennifer laughed at her husband's pink nose, calling him Rudolph. Alessandra helped brush the snow from her brothers' shoulders before she pushed them toward an empty table marked "Reserved."

It was just the same, Scott thought with a mix of relief and elation. Preserved perfectly, like a dream waiting for Scott to drift back into it.

The *it*, Scott also knew—that is, the *it* that was just the same—wasn't Ruby's Place. It was Christmas. It was warmth and togetherness and the sense of truly belonging to one another. It was joy. It was the feeling that the year stretched ahead would be the best any of them had ever had.

The pine in tiny clusters on each table smelled fresh and clean. Chandeliers tossed a glittering light across everything, the soft glow making even the oldest of faces look young again. The ivories on the old upright were already being tickled; those nearest Scott were already humming along. Angela dipped behind the bar—that same heavy, carved, wooden bar that Gregory had remembered fondly. It had been rescued from storage, spiffed up, resurrected. The entire establishment smelled of prime rib and something sweet.

What *was* that? The sweet smell. So familiar.

Scott stopped abruptly, bringing his hands away from the coat rack he was about to prop Jennifer's coat on.

"That's not homemade marshmallows, is it?" he shouted at Angela, who beamed.

"It wouldn't be Ruby's Place on Christmas Eve without homemade toasted marshmallows and cocoa."

"It can't be," Scott said. Only, didn't this seem like something that just happened a few moments ago? Hadn't he had a taste of this treat with his father? Wasn't the inside of his mouth a little scorched?

"Ruby's own recipe," Angela went on. "Get some for the kids?"

"Get—ah—" Scott shook his own questions away and tried his best to smile at Angela. "Get some for *me*," he corrected. All around him came the sound of tinkling glasses, happy voices, laughter. The piano thundered with recognizable chords. All together, the crowd began to sing, "Have Yourself a Merry Little Christmas."

Scott rested his forearms against the bar, his heart full, his eyes threatening to glisten over, so glad he'd come.

As he leaned against the bar, Angela lunged forward and grabbed his hands. "Thank you," she said.

"For what?"

She cocked her head. "You know for what."

"Ang, I just gave you some cash. Not even gave. Loaned. You did the rest."

"But I never would have gotten started—"

Scott tried to wave her away, but she wouldn't let go. Not yet. "Aunt Elizabeth used to tell me how grateful she was for Walter. I mean, everyone says money can't buy you—happiness or love—but that's kind of short-sighted, isn't it? You can't fulfill any kind of dream without it. Someone investing in you—it's huge."

Scott shifted, uncomfortable beneath the weight of all her gratitude. "Look, Ang," he told her, "it was no risk."

Really, it was true. And it had nothing to do with some magical box (of all ridiculous things) in that story he'd imagined Walter telling him. Now that the fog was clearing, he could hardly believe the wild dream he'd gotten from that swift knock in the head. But *Angela*…Scott had encountered his fair share of disappointments and exaggerators and out-and-out liars on the opposite side of his desk at the bank. But he'd always known that Angela would never be one of them. Angela would be the follow-through sort. Because he'd also known how important Ruby's Place was to her. She would never let Ruby's Place down.

"Let me pour this quick drink first," Angela told him, her face flushed. "Then I'll get your marshmallows."

She grabbed a squat glass and poured a scotch neat.

Scott held his breath.

But the arm that reached forward to pick up the glass was not his father's.

"Hey, there, Scott," Brian Young said, winking.

Scott's face fell.

"Sorry," Brian shouted over the din. "Didn't mean to disappoint."

"No, it's just—my father used to drink those," Scott said, pointing at the glass.

"Yeah? I was invited tonight by an old friend of your dad's." Brian raised his glass toward Peter Collins and his wife.

Scott was still in the midst of waving at the couple when Brian barked into his ear, "Listen. I wanted to talk to you. About buying the old Bonwit place."

Scott shivered. "Bonwit?" he repeated. His brain felt a little fuzzy still. But why would someone mention Bonwit out of nowhere? On this night?

"I was looking for a room and happened by the old place," Brian explained, pointing again toward the couple. "Peter over there told me—" He frowned. "That's funny," he said. "Peter was right there. I wonder where he got off to."

When he turned back toward Scott, he shrugged.

"Bonwit," Scott pressed.

"Right. Peter was telling me about Mrs. Bonwit. About how he'd been shooed away from her house. How she used to get after him for cutting through. Taking a shortcut."

"He did?"

"Mmm-hmm. Told me all about it. He wasn't the only one who endured the wrath of Mrs. Bonwit. Sounds like his childhood best friend got some of the worst of it. *And,* as it turns out," he added, nudging Scott with his glass-filled hand, "that best friend was your father. But you probably already knew that, right?"

Scott couldn't speak. Yesterday, he would have sworn he'd never heard that story, not once. Not the one about being chased away from the Bonwit property. Had the seeds been planted by what Gregory had said in his office, and he had filled in the rest of the blanks on his own? How could Scott have dreamed up the exact same story Peter just told Brian?

Had Walter mentioned all this about Bonwit? Had it been a story Scott had been told ages ago, that had somehow bubbled up to the surface after being clocked in the head?

Seemed a little like an old soap opera storyline. The kind of thing that had once kept his grandmother glued to the TV screen when he was a kid. Soap opera characters were the only ones who got memories erased or renewed from being hit in the head. In the real world, a person mostly just got a concussion.

"I want to buy it," Brian said. "The Bonwit house. Turn it into something wonderful. I mean—the house *is* wonderful. Peter let me see the inside and…I'm filled with this sense I could make it into something that would benefit the town. Maybe a B&B. That's what I thought it was to begin with—why I stopped in the first place. It would be good if Sullivan had a place of its own where travelers could spend the night. Wouldn't it?"

Scott only stared at him. He couldn't figure out what to say.

"I'll be staying in the area the next few days," Brian said. "I did want to spend the holiday here. Even if that means staying in a hotel down the highway."

Still, Scott just stared.

"At any rate, I know you have my contact info at the bank, but in case you find yourself with a little downtime during the holiday…" His voice trailed as he began to search his pockets. "Here's my card," Brian said, pulling one from his wallet and dropping it into the side pocket of Scott's suit jacket.

And then, before Scott could quite get a grip on himself, Brian disappeared into the crowd.

25.

DECEMBER 25, 2018
OFFICIALLY CHRISTMAS

A funny thing about that time of day—nearly two in the morning—it was neither late nor early. It was an odd space of time, that blink at which one thing was winding down and another was beginning. It was Christmas. It had officially arrived—not loudly, blaring its horn and revving its engine, but peacefully, like an arm draping itself around your shoulder.

Angela's lucky hat lay in a crumpled mess on the bar, surrounded by a few damp bar towels and her own recently-emptied glass.

The only people left inside were Angela and her crew of two, friends of hers who had agreed to work the opening night for free—and in exchange for all the marshmallows and drinks they could handle, of course.

"You have to let us help clean," Rob pleaded.

"What for?" Angela asked. She pointed at Rob's high school flame, the same that had sparked and started to burn a second time, here in their middle age. "Geena's bussing the last of the tables now."

Geena winked at Rob as he rushed to scoop the giant plastic tub from her, carry it toward the dish area in the back.

When he returned, he found Angela thanking Geena for everything she'd done. There was talk of a cleaning crew, one that Angela had already hired to arrive bright and early on the morning of the twenty-sixth. Yes, the day *after* Christmas had been set aside for the spick-and-span, for taking down the red and green decorations. And, of course, later that day, as the sun went down, Angela would turn her Open sign toward the street for the second time. "Got to think about gearing up for New Year's now," Angela was saying.

In the meantime, a day off for the holiday. A day to relish the silver shine of what had happened on Christmas Eve.

"Well, Rubes," Walter said, settling into a table in the back corner, "I suppose that's your second opening night success. Or should I say 'our'?"

"Yes," Ruby agreed, tapping her champagne flute against the edge of Walter's scotch glass. After such a hectic night, strands of Ruby's hair had worked themselves loose from her bun and hung limply about her jawline. "Although," she admitted, "it's sort of sad to see someone else at the helm."

Her eyes grew a bit misty as she watched Angela hug Rob and Geena goodnight.

"You don't mind *Angela* taking over, surely," Walter

told her.

"Oh, I love Angela. I always did. But—this is my place, Walt. I created it. It's hard to pass it on to someone else."

She shot a look at Walter. "You think I'm being selfish," she guessed.

"Absolutely not," Walter told her. "I was right here for all those years of shooing potential investors away. I know how you couldn't stand the idea of anyone turning this place into a—"

"—soul-sucking office?" Ruby finished with a shudder.

Walter chuckled. "I happened to spend my entire working life in an office. I liked it quite…" His voice trailed.

"What is it?" Ruby asked, but as soon as she glanced through the front window, she saw him. Scott, who had left earlier, but was now back.

He walked up the sidewalk, waving to Rob and Geena, the two friends of Angela's who had just stepped outside.

"Did you forget something?" Geena asked, her voice muffled but still audible through the large front plate glass window.

"I—" Scott offered a strange, painful smile.

"Where's the rest of the family?" Rob asked, apparently trying to rescue Scott as he struggled to put the reason for his return into words.

"Home," Scott said, pointing to some vague location behind his shoulder. "The kids, you know—they were wiped out. Needed to go to bed, so I dropped them and my wife off."

"What made you come back?" Geena asked.

Scott shrugged. "I remembered it all so fondly. And it made me feel so—I don't know—close to the old times that…"

"That what?" Geena pressed.

"I wanted to come in case maybe people were still here. I was hoping there was time, but—it's wound down now, hasn't it?"

"Yeah, Angela's already locked up," Rob said.

Scott's breath made clouds as he turned his face toward the warm red neon sign. "My dad used to bring me here when I was a kid. And tonight, for some reason…"

Inside the bar, Walter felt himself tense up a moment.

Scott laughed it all off dismissively. "The Christmas spirit can get to you, I guess."

He started to back up. "I really should go home. Technically, Christmas Eve has become Christmas morning. Merry Christmas, you two."

Ruby nudged Walter. "Maybe rules are for breaking."

"What, I should run outside and talk to Scott again?"

"He seems to want to talk to you," Ruby reasoned.

"We all promised," Walter said, referring to the agreement the regulars had made. "Once. Every single last one of us regulars, we *all* said we would reach out to a specific loved one once. That way, the past doesn't die, but it doesn't overshadow the present."

"…and besides, it's the mystery and the *maybe* of it all that will keep the customers coming back again and again," Ruby recited, in a feigned low voice, mimicking Walter.

"A promise is a promise," Walter said. "And I aim to keep mine. Besides, I was one of the lucky ones. I got to see two important people tonight. My son and my old friend. My very best friend, from childhood."

He pulled himself from his chair. "It's a beautiful thing, knowing that someone remembers you fondly. To know that you were a high point in someone's life."

"Yes," Ruby agreed, her eyes ever mistier. "It is."

Walter shrugged himself into his coat and propped his hat on at a slant. "Now, if you don't mind," he added gathering up a zippered money pouch, "I have receipts to put back in the vault."

"Receipts," Ruby scoffed. "Still talk in money terms, after all this time."

Walter winked, unable to argue that point. He held on to Ruby's gaze a moment, working up the courage to finally ask, "Did you happen to see her?"

"Who, Hetty?" Ruby asked. "Why would she come? She never wanted to be around anyone in life, to hear you tell it."

"I'd hoped—"

"That she—and possibly her husband, too—could see what it all became? The three little dollars?"

"Yes."

"That, selfishly, you might have even liked a bit of a pat on the back for making sure the magic kept going all these years?"

"Yes."

"And also, you were looking forward to a few answers to questions you've had since you were a ten-year-old kid in Mr. Pulcheck's office? Like where that box came from originally and how it could really contain such magic?"

"*Yes.*"

Ruby snickered. "Doesn't look like you're getting any of that tonight, friend. Guess the mystery will keep *you* coming back, too."

"I suppose it will," Walter agreed. He picked up his scotch glass. "To the ghosts of Christmas past," he said, before knocking the last of it back.

"Merry Christmas to my favorite regular," Ruby told him.

"I get the feeling you've called *all* the regulars your favorite, at some point," Walter said.

Ruby laughed. "See you tomorrow at happy hour."

And she disappeared into the darkened corner.

Walter had somewhere to be himself. But he glanced around for one more good look. Would there even be a happy hour for him to come back to next Christmas Eve? Or would the bank be torn down? Would the vault, the keeper of Sullivan's most powerful items—which is to say, its magic—be destroyed, along with everything inside it?

It was in Scott's hands now.

26.

SCOTT WAVED GOODBYE to Geena and Rob from the driver's side of his car. But he didn't get any farther than putting the key in the lock. He couldn't make himself turn it. Or open the door. Or start the engine.

He couldn't make himself go home yet.

He glanced up and down the street, every single business now a darkened, sleeping storefront. Even Ruby's. The only car left was Scott's. Everyone—even Geena and Rob— had officially left. Most, he figured, were already snuggled in their beds with their sugarplums.

Scott tugged the key out of the door lock and wandered down the street, his topcoat flapping in the December wind, his feet crunching into the snow that continued to fall. Alone, Scott shuddered against the cold. His head had stopped throbbing, but every so often, he reached up to touch his hairline, almost as though to find out if the injury was still there.

He couldn't make sense of what had happened to him that night, and now, with Ruby's closed, he had the feeling he never would.

He paused to touch a strand of tinsel wrapped around one of the streetlights. At least the night had been a success for Angela. She deserved it.

The bank loomed up ahead. A faint light spilled from one of the windows, all the more apparent now against the backdrop of the blackened street. It appeared to be coming from his office.

"Gregory," he muttered. Must've been in too big of a hurry to double-check the lights were all off. For someone who had initially acted as though attending the big reopening was no big deal—not much more than an afterthought—Gregory had certainly enjoyed himself that night. He'd devoured more food than half the crowd, and had belted carols like he thought he was Frank Sinatra incarnate.

Scott unlocked the bank and beelined for his office. He leaned through the open doorway, reaching for the light switch on the wall, when the sight of his desktop caught his attention. He'd cleaned the entire desk off before heading home to pick up his family.

Now, something sat in the center of it.

He drew his hand from the switch and approached his desk.

What was it—an envelope? Yellowed with time?

A hastily-written note left on top was from Gregory. His handwriting was quick and messy, but it said something about finding the letter in a lawyer's office downstairs. "Who is Pulcheck?" Gregory scrawled. "And why has no one ever moved in?"

"Pulcheck?" Scott repeated to the empty office. The basement had an unused office? This part of the story was true, too? Pulcheck's name was still on the door? Why didn't he know that?

Scott tore into the letter. His heart lurched as he recognized his father's handwriting. His eyes scanned the contents quickly, zeroing in on the numbers scrawled along the bottom of the page. Pieces of the night floated back to him—the story Walter had told him of the box—the memory bank.

The vault.

"It can't be," Scott muttered, but he was already bolting for the vault, anyway. His fingers trembled as he worked the combination, spinning the numbers in the order written at the bottom of Walter's letter. He grabbed the handle, but it refused to budge.

His raspy breathing rattled right along with the old letter he shook in frustration. He tried again, spinning the dials, past zero, back the other way.

He took a deep breath and tried a second time.

The door popped.

He wondered how his legs were even carrying him upright as he stepped into the vault. It was empty, of course. No one at the bank would have sealed it up without emptying it first.

Scott turned the letter over, looking for anything that might tell him what to do next. Glancing up at a sea of safe deposit boxes, he spied one with a paper label.

He took a few steps closer, until he could make out his father's handwriting: "Memories of Ruby's. Collected 12/24/18."

It couldn't be. Walter had not lived to see 2018. Maybe the handwriting had smudged? Maybe that was a 7 instead of a 1?

But when Scott squinted, he noticed a second line on the label, also in Walter's handwriting: "To be opened next year—12/24/2019."

It couldn't be real. And yet—it was.

A fresh wave of reason found Scott, and he laughed at himself. "Oh, yeah, dear old dad is still around, hanging out in his favorite bar, collecting the memories every Christmas Eve and then re-releasing them so that everyone will get all nostalgic and come out to Ruby's Place?"

Yes, that was truly the most ridiculous thought he had ever let bounce around the inside of his skull.

"You really did get hit harder than you thought," he told himself.

But even while he was still forming these words, his eyes fell on a second safe deposit box, also with a label. This one already had two keys sticking out of it—the one that remained at the bank and the one that stayed with the owner of the box. The label between the two keys, also in his father's hand, bore his name: "Scott Drummond."

"Okay, this is just ridiculous," Scott said. "Is someone messing with me? Gregory? Gregory!"

No one answered.

Not that Scott really expected anyone to.

"Deep breath and turn," he told himself as he grasped hold of the keys and slid the box free.

Money. The thing was filled with money. Five bundles, to be exact. In the banking world, a bundle was a specific amount of money. And there it was, all cinched together properly, in ten equal straps. All one hundred dollar bills. In one glance, Scott knew he was looking at a half a million dollars. More, actually, than he had loaned Angela.

He heard her all over again, thanking him for what he'd done for her. For giving her dream wings.

And he knew, deep down, that something special had happened to them all that night. Not just to Angela. Something precious. Something light and sweet and full of hope. Some part of all of them had come back, right along with their memories.

In the back of the safe deposit box, beneath the bundles, something sparkled at Scott.

He reached inside and retrieved a strip of tinsel, bright as an entire constellation of stars.

"Okay, Dad, I hear you," Scott whispered. He fished a business card out of his pocket. He was already dialing Brian's number as he let the vault door swing shut and lock into place.

"Mr. Young," Scott said. Using his most professional tone, he said, "I apologize for the late hour, but I had to call you while it was all still fresh in my mind. I was a bit…out of sorts earlier, but I've been thinking of what you said in Ruby's Place. About how you would like to discuss the Bonwit home. I would prefer to discuss something else—a mutually beneficial deal, actually. I believe we can get your company in on it. The money for the Bonwit restoration is yours. Every single cent you need to turn it into a top-notch property, something to benefit the town of Sullivan, something…" Scott's mind spun as he searched for the right word. "Something inviting," was what he came up with.

"Yes," he went on, "you heard me right. No, I'm not drunk. You get the Bonwit home and the funds you need. In return, the Bank of Sullivan will not be torn down. Renovated—I agree with you it does need some work—but renovated in a way that preserves its history. And the old vault. That vault must remain."

Scott paused to listen to a now wide-awake Brian, and smiled. "Yes," he said, "I think we can, too. Thank you, Mr. Young. Perhaps we can discuss this soon. Before you leave town. Why, yes, the bank will open on December 26. Bright and early. I can see you then."

Scott dropped his phone back in his pocket, smiling to himself in satisfaction. He whistled a strange little tune—some sort of mash-up that drifted back and forth between about three different carols—and headed straight for his office, where he picked his tiny tree up off the edge of his desk.

And wove the piece of tinsel from the safe deposit box around its branches.

"Look at you," he said, raising the tree up, where the miniature string of tinsel could catch the moonlight drifting through his window. "You sparkle like a new promise. Let's go home. What do you say? I think you might fit right in the center of our kitchen table. A nice centerpiece for Christmas morning breakfast."

In the lobby, Scott looked all around. And into the empty space, he whispered, "Merry Christmas, Dad."

He stepped outside, into the cold that felt not quite so cold anymore. And in that brief moment before the old bank door fell shut behind him, he could have sworn that he heard a very familiar voice say, softly, "Merry Christmas, son."

27.

APRIL 25, 2019

PETEY LEANED AGAINST the fence outside of the old Bonwit place. The black wrought iron spikes poked at him as he draped his arms over the top.

"So they're really going to renovate it," Petey said, marveling at the construction crew crawling all over the outside of the home. Almost like ants carving away at the farms he'd bought his kids when they were little.

"They're really going to renovate it," Walter agreed.

"Thanks to Scott," Petey finished.

Walter nodded.

"So it's his job to give out the money, and it's your job to collect the memories and release them from the vault each Christmas Eve, keep everybody coming to Ruby's Place for the holiday. Because as long as the memories are alive, so are we."

"That's the idea," Walter said.

"Think Ruby will mind me coming next Christmas?"

"Of course not," Walter insisted.

"But I didn't come for so many years."

"You came last year," Walter said.

Petey worked his jaw back and forth. He ran a hand through his floppy brown hair, styled as he once had when he had first met his wife. "Yeah. But that was different."

"I keep telling you to show up for happy hour with the rest of us regulars."

"Doesn't feel right to be there without my sweetheart," Petey said, staring up at his own home, where his wife sat on the front porch, rocking in a chair and reading a book. Her white hair, piled on her head, looked almost blinding in the summer sun.

"Well, you have to come to happy hour, because I'm putting you in charge of this," Walter said, handing a small wooden box to him. "There are far too many memories anymore to fit in that thing. But I can't let it go."

"What is this thing really, you think?" Petey asked, turning it over in his hands. "I mean, how can it work for memories and money both?"

"I think its magic is to take something small, some minuscule little thing—which is how all good things start, minuscule—and make it bigger."

"Any good thing?" Petey asked. "*Not* just memories or money?"

"I think so, yes," Walter said. "I have no proof, of course."

"Yet," Petey corrected him.

"Yet," Walter agreed.

"You ever think it's weird that suddenly the memories and the money could just take off on their own, grow even outside of this thing?"

"Isn't that always the true magic? That something good cannot be contained? Whether it's love or dreams or the Christmas spirit? Once it has momentum, it just keeps going…and going…"

"So this is how Mr. Bonwit had planned to take care of Hetty from the grave," Petey said, running his hand along the smooth top of the music box. "This old thing that doesn't look like it could have had a drop of magic in it."

"Now, we have to decide what we're going to put in it next," Walter said.

"What we want to get bigger," Petey mused.

Walter nodded.

"I was just thinking," Petey said, glancing up at his house one more time, "about how I had this big life with my sweetheart up there. And it started with the two of us looking at each other in line at the movie theater. Could have been nothing. But we let it get bigger and bigger. Now, it's big enough to hold four grandchildren, six great-grandchildren."

Walter nodded. "Which is exactly why I thought you'd be the perfect person to hold on to that," he said, pointing to the broken music box. "You know all about growing big things."

"I dunno," Petey said. "I kind of feel like I was too rotten to old Mrs. Bonwit to get this now."

"We were all rotten to Mrs. Bonwit," Walter said. "Besides, I only got the box because your dad gave my name to Mr. Pulcheck. And you were the first person I ever tried the magic out on. Seems only fitting that you should have the box now. Friendship seems to be a thing that grows—just keeps multiplying."

"You sound like my grandfather with that corny stuff,"

Petey grumbled.

He turned the box over in his hands. "Maybe there's something to put in here that can remedy the way we were toward Mrs. Bonwit."

"What, call Mrs. Bonwit to town?"

Petey shrugged. "Maybe. Been pretty long, though. Since '38. Where do you think she's been all this time?"

Now it was Walter's turn to shrug. "Maybe with her husband."

"I hope so," Petey said, turning his eyes yet again toward his old porch.

"At any rate, we have to decide what we want to grow from here on out," Walter said. "And there's no time like tonight."

"Tonight?"

"Right. Happy hour. With the rest of the regulars." Walter took a step toward the street. But he stopped, turned back toward his old friend. "Aren't you coming?"

"I want to go inside," Petey said, jabbing a finger at the old Bonwit place.

"You said you didn't ever want to."

"No. I do. I want to go," Petey insisted, even though Walter noticed he was trembling a bit as he pulled away from the fence.

They slipped inside, past the work crews and the hammering and the shouting. They avoided the missing boards in the floor, where a contractor pointed, telling Brian something about rot. A man clattered by, his tool belt loaded and some sort of insulated cable draped in a coil over his shoulder. An electric saw spun. Feet clumped.

Petey tilted his head back to look at the crystal chandeliers, the arched doorways, leaded glass. Window seats in the dining room. Wood floors. Carved newel posts. The marble fireplace.

"It's—just a house," Petey said. "A nice one, but—a house."

"Of course," Walter told him.

Petey squatted down to get a better look at a metal piece just laying on the floor—an old lock, it turned out. A deadbolt. With the key sticking out of it.

"Just think," Petey said, "this place will be full of people. Always an open door. A lock no more."

Walter considered this, his eyes rolling over Petey. Something had happened to his old friend in the moment it took to walk inside the old Bonwit place.

"So much wasted time being afraid," Petey murmured. "So much time behind locked doors."

Walter could tell, by the look on his friend's face, that he knew what he wanted to put in the music box. What he wanted to begin to grow for the people of Sullivan.

Sure enough, Petey glanced about to make sure the contractors weren't watching, and he pulled the key from the lock.

He placed it inside the box.

At that moment, the patina of fear began to dissolve. Dark corners throughout the entire interior of the home began to disintegrate, almost like an invisible hand was scrubbing away at the tarnish left by so many bad feelings—Mrs. Bonwit's apprehension, the children's anger, a neighborhood's avoidance.

The house began to glow from the underneath.

And still, the workers continued on, unfazed.

"Don't they see it?" Petey asked, awe saturating his voice.

"They might not. But they'll feel it," Walter said.

"Look at that," one of the construction workers shouted.

"Maybe they *do* see—" Petey started. But he stopped when he realized the contractor was pointing to something on the opposite side of the living room window. Something in the yard outside.

Walter and Petey turned to look, as did the rest of the work crew.

Snowflakes danced among the budding trees in a rare spring snowstorm, turning the Bonwit place into the welcoming Christmas card it seemed it was always intended to be.

I'll be writing another installment next year, of course. Check *HollySchindler.com* for the latest—or subscribe to my newsletter, so you'll be notified of the latest Ruby's Place publication.

In the meantime, you can read the original four-book Ruby's Place Christmas Collection, which begins when Angela finds herself stumbling onto the past, and deciding that the very best Christmas present would be one more moment spent with a long-lost loved one. She soon learns that at Ruby's Place, the "spirits" are not confined to the dusty liquors behind the bar, and that the Christmas wish to see a special someone one more time is never made in vain.

Or, check out the previous books in the Ruby's Regulars spinoff series. Find out how it was, exactly, that Ruby decided to return home to open the magical supper club. And delve into the stories of her favorite regulars.

All books are available from the same site where you downloaded Tinsel Town.

HOLLY SCHINDLER

Holly Schindler is a critically acclaimed and award-winning author of books for readers of all ages. Her books have received starred reviews in PW and Booklist, and won both the silver medal in Foreword INDIES Book of the Year and the gold medal in the IPPYs. This holiday season, she is drinking too much coffee, singing carols far too loudly, and dreaming up her next Christmas at Ruby's installment.

To find her socials, subscribe to her newsletter, and learn the latest, visit HollySchindler.com.

www.ingramcontent.com/pod-product-compliance
Lightning Source LLC
Chambersburg PA
CBHW020823190726
48285CB00006B/2378